THE ENCHANTERS

The Ocean's Magic

THE ENCHANTERS
The Ocean's Magic

Makayla Sperle

ASA PUBLISHING CORPORATION
AN INNOVATIVE OUTSOURCE BOOK PUBLISHING HYBRID

ASA Publishing Corporation
An Accredited Hybrid Publishing House with the BBB
www.asapublishingcorporation.com
25 S. Monroe St., Suite 203 – Executive Branch, Monroe, Michigan 48161

Copyrights© 2023, Makayla Sperle, All Rights Reserved
Book Title: The Enchanters *The Ocean's Magic*
Date Published: 09.08.2023
Edition: 1, *Trade Paperback*
Book ID: ASAPCID2380878
ISBN: 978-1-960104-07-6
LCCN: Cataloging into Publication

This book was published in the United States of America.
Great State of Michigan

Table of Contents

Chapter 10

Chapter 11

Chapter 12

Chapter 13

Chapter 14

Chapter 15

Chapter 16

About The Author

THE ENCHANTERS

The Ocean's Magic

Makayla Sperle

CHAPTER 1

I CAUSE A CLASSROOM FLOOD

The flood was an accident. At least, it was the first time.

Maybe it was a good thing, maybe it wasn't. All I know is, if I hadn't caused it, none of this would've happened. The original flood is the backbone to everything.

And, of course, me.

Evelyn Autumn, the girl with the water.

It's been a rough couple of years. I've had high times and I've had low times. Times when I thought the world had ended. Times when I thought I was walking on air.

So where should I start?

The answer is obvious. At the beginning, when I first met the Enchanters. Before I knew what I was. Before I became what I am today.

It's a long story, so sit back and relax. Or don't, whatever you prefer. Because, personally, I haven't been able to sleep properly for years. There's always the fear that I will wake up and something terrible will be hunting me down again.

It was the last day of November, and that day it was snowing outside. I was in seventh grade at Eastwood Middle School, living in a small town in southeast Michigan. It was a nice area, with plenty of lakes and pools around to swim in during the summer.

Did I mention I liked swimming? When you live in the state known for its lakes, you do quite a bit of swimming. Anyway, that's not important.

That morning, I woke up before my alarm went off. Since I am very much an early bird, I decided to read a little bit before I had to get ready for school.

Well, that's what I thought.

I had just gotten to a really good part in it when I heard my mom yelling my name from downstairs. I looked up and caught a glimpse of my clock. It read six thirty-seven.

My alarm was supposed to go off at six-thirty . . .

Uh-oh.

I hated ending on a cliffhanger, but I didn't really have a choice. I quickly stuck my bookmark in the book, rolled out of bed, and began getting speed-dressed.

"Evelyn? Where are you? We're going to be late!" my mom called.

"Hold on! I'll be down in five minutes!" I called back.

I ran into the bathroom, brushed my teeth as fast as I could, then ran back to my bedroom.

As I was grabbing my backpack, I glanced out the window.

Standing there, ankle deep in the snow on my lawn, was a figure in a long, dark robe.

"Evelyn?" My mom ran into my room.

My mom, Scarlet Autumn, was an amazing woman in her late thirties. With my same long, curly brown hair and bright blue eyes, we were often told we looked alike. She was smart too, and a really kind person. Just don't mess with her when she is nervous or stressed.

"We need to go! We're going to be—" She stopped when she noticed the person outside the window. I could see how worried she was. It was almost like she knew this strange person.

My dad, Logan Autumn, walked in then. He was slightly taller than my mom, and had brown eyes instead of blue. He was quite known for his dad jokes, which got worse as I got older.

"Are you ready for your English test?" he asked me.

My mom looked at him. "They're here."

His eyes got wide and he looked out the window. I had a feeling I wasn't going to be getting any dad jokes that day. In my opinion, that was actually a good thing.

"Yup, that's them," he told her.

Then he looked at me with intense eyes. "Are you packed for school?"

"Um . . . yeah," I replied uneasily. I was really worried then. Not that I wasn't before. I mean, if a person in a robe shows up on your lawn, then you're going to be at least a little concerned.

"Then we need to go, now," my mom said.

We flew down the road toward the school.

"Who's that?" I asked her nervously.

"Do me a favor and forget you saw them."

"But . . . but who are they?"

"I'll explain later."

I hated those words.

In my first hour math class, I sat by myself. There wasn't anyone who wanted to sit by me. I was just the weird girl with an obsession for reading.

That day, I couldn't concentrate on what I was doing. I kept glancing outside the window, expecting to see that weird person again.

At one point, my math teacher called on me and asked me what the answer to a problem was. I had a really intelligent answer. "Uh . . . um . . . I don't know?"

"You don't know?" She frowned in disappointment.

"I know!" called a boy from the back row.

She sighed. "Kevin, please raise your hand before answering a question."

"Okay, I will, Miss."

I looked outside the window again. The snow was swirling around, and it reminded me of how the currents flow in the ocean.

I really wanted to go to the beach. It would've been a lot more fun than sitting in this classroom. But it was the middle of winter, so that wasn't happening anytime soon.

When the bell rang, I was very thankful. I was ready to leave. Ever since I had given her my "really smart" answer, my teacher kept glancing back at me and frowning.

I stood up to go and she called me forward to her desk.

"Um, yes?" I asked carefully.

"What happened today? You're usually a pretty good student."

"I don't know, ma'am."

"Did something happen? Do you need to visit one of the school's social workers? Your student plan says you can–"

"No, I'm perfectly fine," I assured her.

Something I should probably mention is that I'm autistic, so I have access to some of those things. My teachers and parents knew, but I had always had trouble making friends, so there wasn't anyone else who knew about it.

"Well then, try to pay more attention, and remember there's always the option if you need it."

"Okay, I'll keep that in mind."

"And tomorrow, when you come back to my class, I expect you to be ready to learn, okay?"

"Okay, I . . . I will."

Little did I know, I wouldn't be at school the next day.

In social studies, I had finally gotten my mind off the strange person when I got distracted by a bird sitting on a tree outside. (I get distracted very, very easily. Don't judge me.) Then, the same person appeared outside of the window.

"AGHH!" I yelled. It was almost like they had materialized out of thin air. But that wasn't possible.

Or was it? I thought. *This kind of stuff happens all the time in those books you read.*

Everyone else in the class jumped out of their seats.

My teacher glared at me. "Evelyn, what was that for?"

"Sorry," I said, "I thought I saw something outside."

She sighed. "If you do that again, you will be sent to detention."

"Ooooh," someone cried, "Evelyn's going to be sent to detention!"

"Would you like to be sent to detention?" she asked him.

He was silent the rest of the class.

When the bell rang, I ran out of the classroom. As I walked to my third-hour band class, I told myself that I would forget about the weird individual. It was probably just my crazy imagination. I did have a pretty big one. Or maybe this was all a dream I had subconsciously made up from my love of fantasy books?

I had no idea how wrong I was.

I passed the library, and up ahead, standing in front of the choir room, was my mysterious person.

They were just standing there, in that dark robe with the hood pulled down over their face.

No one else noticed them. Everyone else walked right by them without even looking. Even the teachers paid no attention, and our school had a strict no hats or hoods rule.

Who was that strange person? I still had no clue.

I also had no choice but to go to the band room, which, unfortunately, meant I had to walk right in front of them. Our teachers were also very strict about being late for class. I *definitely* didn't want to get caught skipping.

I snuck past them, trying my best to blend in with the crowd of students pushing each other around. I wasn't a fan of horror movies, (Fantasy is *way* better.) but there was one thing I knew about that stuff:

Seeing things other people can't see is never, *ever* good.

When I reached the door to the band room, I turned around one last time. Was it just me, or had the person moved closer? Without knowing what else to do, I ran into the room, slammed the door shut behind me, and locked it.

Before I can explain what happened, you have to understand what the band room looked like. It was a decent-sized room with fifteen-foot-tall walls that supported the ceiling high above. When you walked in, a door to the right led into the locker area and to the left was our teacher's desk.

In front of that were a few rows of chairs, all facing a small platform. Behind the chairs was the area for the percussionists. (Or, better known, the people that play the drums, but, if you've ever been in a band, you know they are much more than that.) Further behind that was the wall with a single door that was used as a fire escape. Through a window in the door, I could see the snow falling slowly.

Everyone looked up from what they were doing. Some were holding instrument cases, some held instruments, and others just held their books and folders.

I'll admit I was terrified. The only times I had all the attention on me were when I got called down for speech lessons or did something embarrassing.

(Although, the first thing was also pretty embarrassing.)

"Um, what just happened?" asked a flute. (I'm talking about one of the people that plays the instrument, not that the instrument came alive and started talking.)

"Why did you shut the door?" asked a french horn.

"Better question: Why did you lock the door?" piped in a clarinet.

Then everyone else started asking questions at once. I couldn't tell what they were actually saying, but I got the general idea. Over the noise of everyone else talking, I heard someone (I think a percussionist.) yell, "I'll unlock it!"

Sure enough, someone walked over and unlocked the door. A few seconds later, someone else entered. It was our teacher, Mr. Carman.

He walked in to everyone talking and yelled over everyone else's voices. "Quiet down everyone! What's with all the screaming?"

"Evelyn slammed the door and locked it!" one of my classmates yelled.

"Okay now everyone, quiet down and go back to warming up." He raised his eyebrows at me. "Evelyn, come over to my desk with me."

I cautiously followed him back to his desk.

"What happened?" he asked.

"There was a person standing outside the choir room in dark robes! Didn't you see them?"

"What person?"

"I told you, the one in the robe!"

He looked up at me with concern. "Evelyn, are you feeling

okay? Or is this just a joke?"

"I swear it's not," I said, not completely sure myself.

"Look, maybe you need to go home? You're probably just imagining this stuff."

If Mr. Carman truly couldn't see the person, that meant that I was right and only I could see this weird person. My question was: *Why?*

I didn't want to go back out in the hallway by myself, even if it was only for a few minutes to get my stuff. So I told him it was probably my imagination, and I went to go get my instrument.

I got through the warm-up okay, but then the trouble really started.

"Okay, everyone, quiet down." Mr. Carman started, "Today, as I said a few days ago, we will be getting new music."

Cue the talking.

"Please be quiet." Mr. Carman continued, "The new piece we are getting today–"

Bang!!!

The door burst open, and the strange person walked in. Apparently, now everyone else could see them too. They all stared at the person as they walked in, and a few glanced at me. (Probably the ones that had been listening in on Mr. Carman's and my conversation. We had a few eavesdroppers in our grade). He walked halfway into the room and then stopped.

There was silence, which, if you're in band, you know how rare that is in a band room.

"Where is she?" a male voice demanded.

Somehow, I knew he meant me.

I crouched down and hurried over to the percussion area. There, I hid behind the bass drum and listened.

"Where is who?" asked Mr. Carman.

"Evelyn Irene Autumn, the Oceanus."

I didn't have time to question what an Oceanus was. All I cared about was that he was after me.

"Come on out, Autumn" the man ordered, "or we'll curse your band room."

"You will not touch my classroom," Mr. Carman replied.

Curse the band room? What in the world was going on?

All I knew: He wanted *me*, not anyone else.

"Hey!" I yelled, standing up and trying to act threatening. I'm almost a hundred percent sure I failed. "Leave this school *now*."

He chuckled. "Nice, girlie. I can see why you might've been a problem one day. Fortunately for me, it won't come to that. Now, be a nice girl and come gently."

"Evelyn, run!" Mr. Carman pleaded with me.

It's hard to explain what happened next, but all I knew was I wasn't going *anywhere* with that guy.

Suddenly, a warm feeling shot through my body, and I felt

strength and hope and all kinds of other good feelings.

At the same time, the door in the back of the room burst open. The snow (which was suddenly falling very hard now) flowed quickly into the room and instantly changed to water as it did.

Before I knew it, the water was up to my knees.

"What is this?" the man bellowed, "I said come *gently*. I gave you a choice, but if this is how it's going to be, then fine. We can do this the hard–AGHHH!"

A huge wave of water knocked him off his feet, and he was carried out the door on a tidal wave.

The water in the room drained.

After the door slammed shut again, I looked around and saw that all of my classmates were soaked. They were also all staring at me. Then I looked down and realized that I was dry: completely, absolutely, dry.

Mr. Carman looked at me with an urgent expression on his face. "Evelyn, you need to go. Run away. You only made him angry, and he'll come back with more of them with him. Go. Find a guy named Mr. Hunt. He owns a shop in Detroit. You'll know it when you see it. He will be able to help you. Go. And hurry."

Mr. Hunt? What the heck?

But I was being given a chance to escape.

I grabbed my bag and ran out of there.

CHAPTER 2

I MAKE MY ESCAPE

I almost made it.

I ran past the library, and I could see the doors at the end of the hallway.

"You really think you're getting away that easily?"

I turned. Standing there was the man, only now there was another person with him, wearing the exact same thing.

"You can't get away, Evelyn," a female voice issued from under the hood of the other person's robe.

Maybe it's his girlfriend? I thought.

Do you ever wish you could tell your own brain to shut up sometimes?

"Who are you?" I yelled at them, but my voice cracked on the last word.

"We're the Cursers," the man replied.

"You mean the thing that you use to click on stuff on a computer?"

The woman growled. "Ugh! What Enchanter came up with that terrible joke! Have you ever thought about the fact that some words have more than one meaning?"

Enchanters? Who in the world were these people? They were the crazy ones.

"Leave me alone, or I'll . . . I'll flood this hallway!" I shouted at them.

That was an empty threat.

They laughed. "I see what you mean. She is a fiery one," the woman said to the man.

"Come on now," the man said. "Let's try this again. When I say come gently, I want you to come with no screaming and no struggling, okay?"

"No way!" I yelled.

I remembered what it had felt like the first time in the band room, and I imagined the whole hallway flooded with water.

I had no idea what I was doing, but I had no other choice.

"You really want to try messing with us?" the woman asked. "We're not afraid of a little water."

I didn't have a better plan, so I tried to do the best thing I could do until I came up with one. Luckily, I was good at stalling.

I crossed my arms and tried to look intimidating: Which was hard because *intimidating* is not a word usually used to describe me. "Why do you want me so badly?"

"My dear, we were told you are an Enchanter! We had to see this for ourselves."

"Who told you?"

"One of the Speakers! The revealers of the future!" the woman cried.

I didn't even know what an Enchanter was, but, if they were telling the truth and I was one of them, I needed to know.

"What's an Enchanter?" I asked.

"We're not going to let you find out."

"Leave me alone unless you want more tidal wave rides!"

"No, you will come peacefully if you want to survive until tonight," the man retorted.

"We're not supposed to hurt her," the woman told him sternly.

"Fine," he said, "but she won't stop being a big pain!"

"Then we use our magic."

"I can do that."

"What if I act first?" I snapped.

I was tired and confused, but I couldn't let them know that.

"We won't let you," the man replied.

"That's what you think," I retorted.

The same feeling I had felt earlier surged through me, and the windows all along the wall shattered. Water flowed in at speeds of a hundred miles-per-hour and, in a second, the rest of the hallway was flooded. The speed of the water knocked them off their feet.

The water seemed to soak into the ground, and, just as

quickly as it started, it was gone. The Cursers sat up, coughing and gasping for air.

"Once again," I yelled, "leave me alone!"

I turned and ran down the hallway away from them.

"You . . . you won't g-get a-way with th-this," the man coughed.

I turned the corner at the end of the hallway and continued running. Eventually, I found a janitor's closet and ran into it, slamming the door shut behind me.

Then I heard them coming.

"You foolish girlie," the man yelled. "You think you can get away from us?"

"If you think you're so tough, get out here and fight us!" the woman called. "Show us how strong you are! Come on now! Don't be a scaredy cat!"

"Come on out!" the man called. "You showed us your tricks, now let us show you ours!"

Not in a million years, I thought.

"We can't be beaten by a little girl!" I heard the woman tell the man. "If she escapes—"

"I know! We have to find her!"

"This was supposed to be the easy job!"

I listened to their retreating footsteps getting quieter and quieter as they walked down the hallway looking for none other than *me*.

I sat in the closet for a few minutes, twirling a curl of my hair around my finger. I always do that when I get nervous.

I was stuck in a really bad spot. In about half an hour, the bell would ring and everyone would find out what I had done. Which I found really confusing, because I wasn't even sure *what* I had done.

There was only one thing to do. The thing Mr. Carman had told me to do:

I had to run.

I looked around at the stuff in the janitor's closet. Maybe there was something in there that I could use?

I rummaged through the stuff, looking to see what was in there. All I found were mops, buckets, and bottles of cleaning spray.

Then, I found my jackpot.

Apparently the janitor kept his coat in the closet, because, hung up on a hook on the back wall, was a brown jacket.

I took it off the hook and put it on. It was a little too big, but it was better than nothing.

I put my hands in the pockets and pulled out a wallet.

I didn't want to take the whole wallet, so I figured I would just take about fifty dollars or so and leave the rest, right?

The wallet was empty.

Why? I thought. *Just why?*

I set it down on the floor of the closet and continued looking, but I didn't find anything else I could use.

Then it hit me. What was I doing? I couldn't run away. That would be madness!

But I may have just discovered what madness felt like.

So, instead of waiting for someone else to find me, I snuck out of the closet, careful to be quiet. I quickly ran towards the front of the school and figured that they (the Cursers, as they called themselves) would expect me to sneak out the back way, because who in their right mind would sneak out the front?

I would.

After making sure no one was watching, I slipped out the front doors and ran off in the direction the sun set. I had no food, no water, and no money. All I had was some janitor's coat. Not to mention, it was the beginning of winter. It was freezing outside.

Had I lost my mind?

CHAPTER 3

I MEET THE GIRL OF NATURE

When you hear the words "nature girl," you would probably picture a calm girl with a dress made of plants and flowers in her hair.

Parker Thomas was not like that.

After running through the suburbs and cornfields of southeast Michigan for a few hours, I finally came across a small park. The park was surrounded by thick woods with very few hiking trails.

The perfect place for a night's rest.

Luckily, I had found that coat so I wasn't *completely* freezing, but I was still pretty cold.

I walked through the woods until I found a small clearing. There, I found a soft spot on the ground and sat down to think.

I had so many questions.

Who were those people? Why was I being told to go to this place? What was an Enchanter?

Was I going crazy?

Suddenly, I heard noises coming from the left, leaves

crunching and twigs breaking.

Someone was coming.

I grabbed a large stick off the ground and held it like a baseball bat, preparing to attack if I had to.

Then, Nature Girl entered the clearing.

She was about the same height as me, with auburn hair that was pulled back in a ponytail and brown eyes that were slightly hidden behind glasses. Her faded, light blue coat was dirty and her jeans were ripped. Slung over her back was a small drawstring bag. She held a small pocket knife, and it was pointed right at me.

In spite of that, she did not radiate fear. Her face was full of the same confusion and worry I had.

"Who are you, and what are you doing here?" I asked, not lowering my stick.

"I could ask you the same question," she replied. "I bet you work with them?"

"With who?"

"With the Cursers! Those people keep following me! I thought I had lost them!" She glared at me. "And then I found you."

"I don't work with them! They're after me too!"

"A likely story," she said sarcastically.

"I just came here from my school! I don't know how, but I somehow managed to flood my band room and one of the hallways!" I told her.

I didn't fully believe it myself, but I knew deep down it was true. I also wasn't in the mood to fight this girl, and, if she was telling the truth, she was on my side.

I dropped the stick I was holding and held up my hands. "Look," I started, "I'm not with them, okay? I just had a tiring and confusing day. I was followed, I was chased, and I'm running away. My teacher told me where I could get help, but I don't know where I'm going. If you're running away from them too, then maybe we can help each other."

She lowered her knife and considered me for a moment. "I've been running for a week now, and all I've found are people who want to kidnap me." She took out her water bottle. "I've discovered that I can summon fruit for food, but I'm constantly running out of water, and I've had barely any sleep for a week."

"Maybe I can help with that," I said. I stepped forward and put my hand on the empty bottle. It instantly filled up with water.

"You can summon water?" she asked.

"Apparently," I replied. "You said that you can summon fruit?"

"Not just fruit," she said. "I can summon pretty much anything in nature, other than animals."

"So," I said, "I have water, and you have food. Maybe we can work together?"

She shrugged. "I don't see any reason why not. But, if you try to kidnap me, I'm running away."

"Okay, deal," I said, "and I promise I won't kidnap you."

In half an hour, Nature Girl and I (after telling each other our real names) had settled ourselves down. I told her my story, and we discussed where to go next. Neither of us had heard of Mr. Hunt or his shop in Detroit, but it was the only lead we had.

Parker sighed, "You know, I can't remember the last time I sat down and talked to someone. I've just been so busy, you know, running."

"You said it's been a week, but you make it sound like longer."

"Yeah," she said in a daze. "It has only been a week. Feels like longer."

I looked at her and saw that she had a sad look in her eyes. I had the feeling she was hiding something, but I decided not to pry.

"Since I actually got to sleep last night, do you want me to take first watch, Nature Girl?"

She raised her eyebrows. "Nature Girl?"

"Yeah, it's a nickname."

"Uh, no. That's not going to be a thing."

I laughed. "Good night, Parker."

"Good night," she replied. "And I'm not Nature Girl!"

"Whatever you say."

She rolled her eyes at me and lay down. Soon, Parker was snoring. She must have been really tired.

I sat up and looked at the sky through the top of the clearing. I'd had a rough and very confusing day. Even if I had let Parker take the first watch, I was sure I wouldn't have been able to sleep.

In my mind, I replayed a scene from earlier.

"Where is she?" the Curser had asked.

"Where is who?" Mr. Carman had responded.

"Evelyn Irene Autumn, the Oceanus."

How had he known my name? Or where to find me?

What was an Oceanus?

I looked down at Parker's water bottle, which was almost empty again since she had drunk most of it. I wondered . . .

The thing he had called me, an *Oceanus*? The word was like the word ocean, but with the letters 'us' added on to the end. Was that someone who could summon water?

It felt like it had all been a dream, but I grabbed Parker's bottle and filled it up with water.

I dumped it out and filled it with water again. I did this a few more times, each time getting easier and easier.

Practice makes perfect.

But nothing *was* perfect, so I changed it to *practice makes progress*. It still had a ring to it, but it was the truth. You make progress whenever you practice.

Yes, I'm a nerd.

Finally, I set down the water bottle. So it was true: I could summon water with just my bare hands, and Parker . . . Parker could summon nature.

I had always dreamed of having magical powers, but those had always been dreams. I never thought I *actually* did.

In spite of the danger we were in, I couldn't help smiling. When I woke Parker up a few hours later for her watch, I was still grinning like a crazy person.

When I woke up the next morning, I didn't immediately open my eyes. My first thought was that since I hadn't woken up to my alarm, it must either be a Saturday or I forgot to set it again.

Then I remembered what had happened.

My eyes snapped open, and I sat up.

Parker was standing a little ways away from me, waving her arms around and making berry bushes pop up out of the ground. I watched her for a minute before she turned around and realized I was awake.

"What do you want?" she asked. "There's strawberries, blueberries, raspberries–"

"So basically," I summed up, "there's any kind of berries you want."

"Exactly."

"What if I don't want berries?"

"Then get your own breakfast."

"I'm kidding. I'll eat the berries," I told her.

She stopped the whole summoning-berries-thing and picked up her bag. Out of the bag she pulled a small, plastic bowl.

"For the berries," she told me.

"What do you *have* in there?"

"Let's see: I've got my water bottle, the bowl, twenty dollars, my pocket knife, matches, my flashlight, and my first aid kit."

"Did you have time to *plan* on running away?"

"First of all, no, I got this from a shop I passed. Second, I don't want to talk about why I ran away."

I decided it was probably best to drop it.

Cleaning up took almost no time at all. It consisted of me filling up the water bottle and Parker getting rid of her berry bushes, which she did with a simple wave of her hand while I stared dumbfoundedly at her.

I was still getting used to the whole magic thing.

"Okay, where to next?" she asked.

"That way," I said, pointing to the northeast. "If we go straight that way, we'll eventually end up in Detroit."

"Okay then." She waved her hand in the direction I was

pointing. "Lead the way!"

By the time noon came around, Parker and I had reached the city of Detroit.

For those of you who have never been to Michigan, let me explain Detroit.

Detroit is a pretty big city. You wouldn't think that just a few miles away was all cornfields and lakes. A lot of the city was broken down or under construction, but it was still cool to see: Tall buildings stretched into the sky, old car factories that were still in business after years of work, a few theaters and hotels.

"Okay, so where do we go from here?" Parker asked me.

"Well, we *definitely* don't want to go that way," I said, pointing, "so let's try that way." I pointed to one of the side roads.

"That road is mostly apartments," she pointed out.

"Hey, we can *summon things*. You never know where something might pop up," I told her. "We have to think outside the box."

"Okay, fine," she shrugged. "I see no other option."

"Then follow me."

We started up the street. It was full of small shops and businesses. It didn't seem like the place where you would find a guy with a magic shop, but I had a weird feeling something was down here.

"Evelyn, I have no idea why I decided to trust you," Parker said. "We are lost in a city I don't know anything about, but, somehow, I *do* trust you. It's weird."

"I get it," I said. "I have the feeling I should trust you, too, but when I first saw you, you looked like you were about to kill me."

"Yeah, sorry about the pocket knife," she said. "You're the first decent person I've met all week."

"Am I *ever* going to get details on why you were on the run this week?"

"What does that sign say?" she asked, ignoring my question and pointing at one of the shops.

I looked where she was pointing, and above an old door was a sign that read:

Mr. Hunt's: Open 10 AM - 5 PM

"That's it!" I said, "Mr. Hunt!"

"So, we just go inside?"

"Apparently."

And so, Parker and I walked into the shop.

Chapter 4

We Finally Get Some Answers

As soon as I entered, I realized something about the items for sale.

None of this stuff belonged in a normal store.

It was a small room, with shelves on either wall filled with stuff for sale. There were colorful jars filled with stuff labeled *Powdered Horn* or *Dragon Scales: Fire-Proof Variety*. In one area, I saw collections of books titled *The Healer's Guide To Burns and Bruises* and *The Speaker's Collection of Prophecies*.

"Wow," Parker said in awe.

"I agree," I replied.

We walked towards the checkout counter in the back of the shop. Standing behind the counter was a guy, probably in his late thirties, with deep blue eyes and blonde hair slicked back.

He smiled at us as we walked forward, and spread his arms in greeting.

"Hello!" he said cheerfully. "Welcome to my shop! I'm Colten Hunt, but you can call me Colten. I assume you guys are young Enchanters since you found my store. Early Magics, I would guess. I haven't seen you two before."

"Early Magics?" I questioned aloud. "We were sent here by my band teacher, Mr. Carman. And, if an Enchanter is someone who can do magic, then yes, we are."

He nodded in respect. "Fast learners. Enchanters are, indeed, people of magic, and an Early Magic is just our nickname for the ones that find out they have magic early."

"See? They use nicknames," I whispered to Parker.

"Be quiet and let him talk."

"But you look older than that," Colten remarked.

Next to me, Parker shrugged. "I get that a lot. That I look older than I actually am."

"Same here," I agreed.

He nodded. "Well then, I guess I have some explaining to do."

The first thing he did was lead us through a door behind the counter (how had I not noticed that?) and into a small room that I assumed was his living room.

It was small but cozy. There was a couch on the left wall that faced a grand fireplace with a TV on top. On the wall that faced us was a tall bookshelf with a small, cluttered desk next to it. Sitting at the desk was a woman about the same age as the man. When we walked in, she turned around and smiled at us.

"Colten? Who are these guys?" she asked.

He smiled at her. "Early Magics."

"I was an Early Magic," she told us. "I'm a Speaker. I can—"

"Tell the future?" I guessed.

She looked impressed. "How'd you guess?"

"One of the Cursers said something about a Speaker."

"You're Evelyn Autumn, aren't you?" she asked, a small grin creeping across her face.

"Um, *yes*."

"And you're Parker Thomas?" She looked at Parker.

Parker nodded, "That's me, and that's kinda creepy."

"You guys have rough days ahead," she told us. "But always remember this: Love is one of the greatest things out there, and you will find plenty where you go. When all hope is lost, just remember the ones you love, and you'll find your way."

"*Okay then . . .* " I said. I hadn't expected the deep love talk.

"In other news," Parker said, "we were told to come here, so I'm assuming you can help us in some way? I mean, other than the talk about the future."

"Of course," she said. "We can take you to Enchantia."

"What's Enchantia?" I asked. "I keep hearing that, Mrs. Hunt."

"Please, call me Ellie," Ellie said, a definite smile on her face. "I prefer using my first name."

"Okay, Ellie." Parker asked again, "What is Enchantia?"

"Enchantia is where all young Enchanters go to learn how to

control and use their magic wisely," she explained. "You stay there during the school year, and then you come home during the summer. Of course, you will still do some of the regular, non-magic classes like english and math—"

"Wait, wait, wait," Parker interrupted, and held up her pointer finger to indicate quiet. "We get to go to a magic school, but we still have to do math? Come on!"

I agreed with her.

Ellie laughed. "Not many Enchanters are fans of that either, but you still have to learn that stuff."

"But it's a *magic school*!" I complained.

"On other topics," Colten said. "Usually how this works is that once you turn thirteen you are taken to Enchantia in the fall to start your time there. However, for some people, you learn about your magic earlier than that."

"Like me," Ellie said. "I discovered my magic when I accidentally said a prophecy aloud in gym class."

"You did?" I asked. "You can really see the future and tell prophecies?"

"Yep," she said, "There are eight different types of Enchanters: the Speakers, who tell the future. The Oceanus, who have water magic. The Flames, who can summon fire. The Windys, who control the air . . . "

"The Forestus control nature," Colten chimed in. "The Sparks control electricity and light. The Freezers control ice and snow. And the Healers, well, that's pretty self-explanatory: They heal."

"That's a lot to remember," I remarked.

"It's easier the more time you spend in Enchantia," Ellie reassured me.

"Still a lot."

"Just remember: prophecy, water, fire, air, nature, electricity, snow, and healing."

"So, anyway, how do we get there?" Parker asked.

"We'll take you," Colten said. "We'll ride in my car to a port on the Detroit river. Then we'll take a boat to the island, which is in Lake Erie."

"Enchantia is an island in Lake Erie?" I asked.

"Yup," Ellie said.

"Then how has no one found it?" Parker questioned.

"There is ancient magic surrounding the island, so that you can only find it if you're with someone who has been there before." She explained, "Once you've been, you can come back whenever you want."

"Cool," I said. "So if we tried to go there on our own, we couldn't find it?"

"Yup," Colten said, "Ellie and I met at Enchantia, and now we help out there whenever we can."

"While you're there, you'll meet other people like you,

children and teens who have magic gifts," Ellie told us. "You may meet your best friends—"

"Or your worst enemies," Colten finished.

"I like the idea of friends," Parker said, "*Not* a fan of the worst enemies."

"Wait," I said, "how do we *get* our powers? I mean, what makes us different from regular kids?"

"Most people inherit the magic from their parents," Ellie said.

"Then how come we didn't know about it until now?"

They both looked at each other and sighed. "There was a law that was passed years ago that parents couldn't tell their kids that they had magic," Colten explained.

"Yeah," Ellie agreed. "It was because of the Cursers. They went around to schools, looking for kids who were using magic. You can't tell a little kid that they have powers without them trying to use them. So once they found a kid with powers, they would, well . . . " She looked at Colten.

"Kidnap them," he finished, "to try to get them to join them. Use their powers for evil."

"That's horrible!" Parker and I exclaimed.

"I know," Colten sighed. "So they made the law, so that kids wouldn't know about their powers and try to use them."

"Why not just tell the kids to not use their powers?" I asked.

"It's harder to control a power you know you have," Ellie

explained. "So sometimes kids would use their powers without meaning to."

"There's got to be another way."

"We're constantly trying to find one," Ellie said. "We just don't know what to do."

"We'll help," I said, "We'll find a way."

"Well, it seems today you are joining the Enchanters," Colten said. "So, for right now, let's find our way to the car."

Ellie stood up. "Let's go! I always love a visit to Enchantia."

We walked outside and climbed in the Hunts' SUV.

Parker insisted that her bag was kept with her, so the bag was squeezed between me and her in the backseat.

"It'll only take a few minutes to drive to the port," Colten explained. "And once we get there, it's just a short boat ride to the island."

I sighed, "I can't wait."

"Well, you have no choice," Parker told me. "Be patient."

But, since I didn't have any patience, I couldn't just sit still and wait. So I decided to try making small talk with Parker. Risky, because that was something I was usually bad at.

"So," I said to Parker. "You're from Chicago?"

"Yup," she said.

"What's it like living in a big city?"

"It's pretty good. When you want to go somewhere, you can just hop on the subway or ride your bike there or just simply walk."

"That sounds cool, but one thing . . . "

"Yes?"

"Why did *you* run away? I told you why I did, but what happened to you?"

"I don't want to talk about it."

"That bad?"

"Yes. We're moving on to another topic," she said with finality.

"Okay, then," I said cautiously, sure I had already messed up big time. "What do you think Enchantia will look like?"

"Maybe it's a big castle?" she wondered aloud. "Or it could be a camp. Or maybe it's an entire hidden village!"

"You mean with blocks of homes and magic shops and tiny restaurants?"

"Yeah," she started to ease up. "Maybe it's a whole city! With tons of people!"

"But I thought parents were forbidden to tell their kids about it?" I pointed out.

"That's true."

We spent the rest of the ride talking about what we thought it would look like. As we talked, Parker got more and more cheerful. Eventually, she was smiling from ear to ear. I was pretty sure I looked the same way. Parker's excitement was contagious.

"Hey, guys," Ellie turned around from the passenger's seat. "Look straight ahead."

I did, and I saw a large, green body of water snaking its way between Michigan and Canada.

"That's the Detroit river," I said, pointing out the window.

"And this," Colten said as we pulled up to a small port next to the river, "is where we get out."

"So," Ellie explained, "when we arrive, you will be introduced to the nine Leaders. The Leaders will be your teachers for the rest of the year. Each one of them covers a different power–"

"Wait," I interrupted, "Nine? I thought there were only eight different powers, and each person only belongs to one."

"Well," Ellie said, "except for Raven Emerald."

"Who in the world is Raven?" Parker asked.

"Every generation, one Enchanter is born with all eight powers. They are known as the Chosen Ones. The Chosen One is basically the boss of Enchantia. They oversee everything that goes on there, and it is their job to protect the school."

"Speaking of Enchantia," Parker said, bouncing up and down on the balls of her feet. "Can we go now?"

Colten smiled at her. "Sure, wait here, and I'll go get us a ride." He ran inside a small building next to the port.

Parker looked up at Ellie. "How long is the boat ride going to be?"

"It should just take a few minutes," she said. "Well, unless we run into any water dragons. They are always looking for someone to play with."

"There are water dragons?" I asked.

She laughed. "There are water dragons. In fact, pretty much any creature you have read about in a fantasy book is real."

"Wait, but then the non-magical people know that those exist."

"Sometimes people see magical creatures and tell other people about them before we can interfere. Have you heard of the Loch Ness Monster?"

"Yeah."

"Nessie is a water dragon. But I hate the fact that everyone thinks she's scary. She's very friendly and playful."

I smiled. "That's really cool."

Colten came out of the building and headed over to where we were standing. He had a huge grin on his face.

"Okay," he said. "There's a boat waiting for us. It's time to go to Enchantia."

CHAPTER 5

WE GO TO ENCHANTIA

For the most part, the boat ride was pretty cool.

It was a nice sailboat with a light aqua-colored sail that reflected the water and enough seats for all of us to sit in.

The only bad part was when Parker's glasses flew off, and Colten, who was also an Oceanus, made them come back into the boat on a wave.

Honestly, I thought the wave thing was pretty cool.

Also, the boat went a lot faster than a normal one, zooming across the water at high speeds.

Suddenly, up ahead, I spotted a small, green thing on the horizon. "Is that it?" I asked, pointing.

Ellie nodded, "Yup, welcome to Enchantia."

Enchantia was beautiful.

There was a beach wrapping all the way around, but, since it was winter, there wasn't anyone on it. Further up on the island, I saw a big, central area where there were snow-covered trees and rocks spaced out. A big fountain was in the middle of it, and a sidewalk wrapped its way around and then split off into different directions. There were kids and teens running around, having snowball fights or building snowmen. On either side of that, there were lots of small buildings spread out, with a sidewalk connecting all of them.

And right in front of us was the biggest thing there.

It was a castle, a real, live castle, with towers that stretched into the sky. I could see tons of balconies and windows. Behind it spread a large forest, and I could see small lights flickering from within it. The entire thing felt, well, magical.

"Wow," Parker and I said together.

"That's amazing!" I said.

"It's beautiful!" Parker exclaimed.

"It is amazing and beautiful, isn't it?" Ellie told us, "That's where you'll spend the next couple of years."

I stared up at the castle and noticed that the tallest tower was glowing. However, I couldn't tell you what color it was because every time I looked it changed.

"What's up there?" I asked, pointing.

"I don't know," Colten said. "Only Raven knows that. Apparently, it's something very powerful."

"Okay, then," I said. "So if this is where we're staying, then where are the actual rooms we will be staying in? I mean, which buildings?"

"That one," Ellie said and pointed to the castle.

"That's where we'll live?" I asked in awe.

"Yup, but they'll explain all that in a minute. The Leaders will take you on a full tour of the island. They'll show you all the classrooms and talk to you about everything you want to know about Enchantia."

We pulled up to a set of docks coming off the beach, and standing on the docks were a group of nine people, each wearing a different colored robe over their clothing.

We stepped up on the dock, followed by Colten and Ellie.

In front of us, one of the nine stepped forward: a young woman with short, blonde hair wearing a golden robe that shone in the sun. She was pretty young, probably only fifteen or sixteen, and younger than the others. But it was clear she was in charge. She had an aura of power surrounding her that none of the others had.

"Welcome to Enchantia," she announced. "I know who you are," she pointed to me, "Evelyn Autumn."

I nodded.

"And Parker Thomas."

Parker just said, "That's me."

"I am Raven Emerald, Leader of Enchantia, the Chosen One of this generation."

"That sounds like a lot of work," I remarked.

She raised her chin towards the sky. "It is a *very* important job. Only one person can do it at a time. But on other topics . . . "

Raven turned around and called forward two people, a man wearing a teal robe and a woman wearing a green one. Other than Raven, they were the two youngest, probably in their early or middle twenties.

"This is Mr. Hudson and Ms. Maple," she told us. "Mr. Hudson is the Leader in charge of the Oceanus, and Ms. Maple is the one in charge of the Forestus. They will be in charge of your magic training, and you will go to them for any questions or concerns you might have. They are our newest recruits, only becoming Leaders last year, but they are amazing at it. Please enjoy their tour, and, for the last time, welcome to Enchantia."

Raven and the other six people in robes walked away, talking, and Mr. Hudson and Ms. Maple stepped forward.

"Evelyn, Parker, nice to meet you," Mr. Hudson said with a smile.

"Yes, and I know you've heard it before, but welcome," Ms. Maple said. "I still remember when I was new here. It seemed so weird. But it's home to me now, and I hope you find as much joy here as I did."

I looked at Raven and the other Leaders walking away and shook my head. "You know, when I was first told about Raven Emerald, I didn't expect her to be so, well, young. She's barely older than me."

"That's because she didn't start that long ago." Mr. Hudson explained. "The way the Chosen One works is that thirteen years before each one dies, another will be born, so that when the current one dies, they are old enough to begin training here. They cannot use their power until the one before them dies, which will happen on that person's thirteenth birthday."

"Well, I guess I'm not that person, since I'm twelve and I have already used my power."

"Same here," Parker agreed.

"It probably won't change again for a long time, since Raven has only been here for three years. Depending on how long you live, it may not even be in your lifetime."

Mr. Hudson turned to Colten and Ellie. "I assume you're going to visit for a little bit, get to see Carly and Austin before you leave."

"Who are Carly and Austin?" I asked.

"Carly is our ten year old daughter," Ellie replied. "And Austin is our thirteen year old son. We only see them during the summer or on the weekends, when parents can come and visit, but we love them. And they're incredible children."

"Now it's tour time," Mr. Hudson announced. "Follow us this way!"

We were shown many things on our tour. It turned out the island was bigger than we thought. Most of the buildings we saw at first were classrooms, but then we were shown everything else.

"What's that building?" I asked, pointing to a small building that sat apart from the others.

"I'll show you," Mr. Hudson told me, and we followed him into the building.

It ended up becoming one of my favorite places there.

It was a pool with eight lanes and a high dive over the deep end. There were a few kids swimming in it, and, when I looked down into the bottom, I was surprised to see two kids sitting down there: just chilling like there was nothing strange about hanging out on the bottom of the deep end.

Obviously, they were both Oceanus.

"Wow, cool," I said.

Mr. Hudson laughed. "You'll spend a lot of time here, especially as an Oceanus. Even the others spend a lot of time here for exercise. Swimming is a great way to work out."

One girl did a flip off the high dive, and a few of the other kids cheered. When the girl came up, she spotted Colten and Ellie and swam over.

"Hey, Mom. Hey, Dad," the girl said, "What are you doing here? It's a Wednesday afternoon! I just got done with my classes."

She was younger than the others I'd seen, with wavy, blonde

hair and brown eyes. She was wearing a one piece blue swimsuit, and, even though she seemed really happy, I could tell by looking in her eyes that she was upset about something.

Once again, I decided not to say anything.

"Carly, this is Evelyn and Parker. They're new here," Ellie explained. "We helped them get to the island."

"They found your shop?" Carly asked.

"Yup," Colten told her.

"I'm not surprised," she replied.

"Do you guys want to stay here while Amelia and I take the girls on the rest of the tour?" Mr. Hudson asked Colten and Ellie.

It took me a minute to realize he was talking about Ms. Maple.

"Sure," they replied.

"Go ahead," Ellie told us.

"Hope to see you guys again," Colten told us.

We said our goodbyes to Colten and Ellie, and Ms. Maple and Mr. Hudson continued on their tour.

The next things we saw included the sports field, the art building, the dining hall, the study hall, the hospital building, and the stables, which were filled with pegasi and unicorns.

It was finally time for us to be shown the castle.

It was nine stories high (not counting the towers, where the Leaders slept) and Ms. Maple explained to us that each of the upper eight floors was reserved for one kind of power. On each floor were things special to that power. Each one also included bathrooms and bedrooms for us.

The doors of the castle were light brown, and on the door was a logo: a capital letter 'E' surrounded by stars.

When we walked in, we were in an open room with a double staircase at the end of the hall leading up to the other floors. In between the stairs was a set of double doors (why was there so much double stuff?) about ten feet tall. On either wall were two fireplaces facing each other. People lounged in chairs and couches spread around the room.

"This is the common area," Ms. Maple explained. "It's where a lot of people like to spend their evenings in the winter."

We walked through the middle of the common area, heading towards the doors. As we walked, people saw us and started whispering to their friends. I could make out the words *"new,"* *"never seen them before,"* and *"wonder what their powers are."*

I tried to ignore the whispering. We were the new kids here, and that always made people talk. You couldn't be the new kid at the school without any rumors about you going around.

We reached the doors, and Mr. Hudson opened them for us.

The room made me completely forget about the whispering.

It was the library, and it was the most amazing library I had ever been in: two stories high, with a balcony that wrapped all the way around the top level. There were bean bag chairs and armchairs to read in and a few desks, in case you wanted to study there. There was a grand fireplace at the end of the room, filled with a blazing warm fire. A small but beautiful crystal chandelier hung from the ceiling.

In other words, it was a book lover's dream.

"Wow," I said in awe.

"You can come in here anytime you want," Ms. Maple told us.

"*Ooooh*! So, *anytime*, as in I could come in here in the middle of the night if I wanted to?"

Ms. Maple laughed. "For the library, yes. You just aren't allowed to leave the castle at night, but you can visit the library and the common area at any time."

"That's cool." Inside my head, I was already planning some late night reading trips.

"How about we get you to your rooms?"

"Yeah, let's go!" Parker said with enthusiasm.

We visited her room first, which was a small room with pastel green walls and real grass for the floor. It felt like you were in the middle of a forest, and Parker screamed with joy when she saw it.

"This is awesome!" Parker exclaimed. "It's like living in nature! How . . . how is this possible?"

Mr. Hudson smiled. "When a new Enchanter arrives, the castle automatically makes a new room that fits their interests. I don't think I've ever seen someone who didn't like their room."

"And . . . it's mine?"

Ms. Maple nodded, "It's all yours!"

"This is amazing!"

Mr. Hudson turned toward me. "Ready to see your room?"

"Definitely," I said.

"Wait!" Parker called, "I want to come too!"

Finally, we reached the top floor, the Oceanus level.

I walked down the bedroom hallway looking for my name, but I couldn't find it. Then I reached the door at the end of the hallway, and read the name:

Evelyn Autumn

I had found it.

With Ms. Maple, Mr. Hudson, and Parker watching me, I reached out and opened the door.

It was amazing. The walls were light blue, with light splashed across them so it felt like you were underwater. The floor was actual sand, but somehow none of it stuck to anything. The bed was simple, just a mattress fitted with yellow sheets (my favorite color), and a nightstand was next to it. There was a desk with a calendar that had pictures of the ocean hanging over it. In one corner was a tall bookshelf filled with my favorite books and ones that had been on my *must read* list.

Then I saw the best part.

There was a glass door that looked out onto a balcony. I ran over, opened it, and stepped out.

Even though it was a freezing winter, I could tell the view would be amazing in the summer. My bedroom was facing away from the central green, and I could see the forest spread out below. The cold waters of Lake Erie swirled in the distance, and, surprisingly, I felt right at home.

I stood there for a minute, just staring at the view, and then I forced myself to walk back inside where everyone else was waiting.

"What do you think?" Ms. Maple asked me.

I smiled. "It's wonderful! I love it!"

"I'm glad," Ms. Maple said. "Now we're going to leave you guys to your new rooms, and we'll see you soon."

She and Mr. Hudson walked out of the room, and I listened as their footsteps grew fainter and fainter.

Parker looked at me. "Well, that was an eventful day."

I nodded, "Yeah, it was."

"What should we do now?"

I thought for a second before answering. "Maybe we should explore on our own now? I mean, sometimes there are things that aren't said in the tours."

"Or there are things that the Leaders don't know about?" Parker thought aloud. "Like, don't a lot of castles have secrets? Things most people never find unless they find it by accident or go looking."

"So, let's go looking!"

Parker grinned. "This is gonna be fun."

CHAPTER 6

THE COVER UP ATTACK

Parker and I stopped by her room first so that she could change into new clothes, and, once she was done, we went outside to explore.

We walked out into the central green, and I joked with her that they should change the name in the winter since it was currently *not* green.

When we reached the fountain we found four people standing there talking. We walked towards them, but they didn't seem to notice us. As we got closer, we could hear their conversation.

"Luna, are you sure it was us?" asked a guy with messy black hair and pale skin. "So far, I'm not a big fan of this vision."

The girl he was talking to, Luna, who had dark hair and skin, retaliated with, "No, Mason, I'm telling you! It was us, all of us, but there were two other girls with us. We were in danger, in some kind of dark hallway or something."

"Okay then," Mason said, "but you know I'm not a fan of creepy dark hallways. Who are these two girls that are with us?

Have you seen them before?"

She shook her head. "Never seen them before."

Another guy, this one with brown hair and wearing a white robe, asked, "Can you describe them? Maybe we've seen them before."

She started describing. "One of them had curly brown hair and blue eyes. She was an Oceanus because she used her powers. The other had auburn hair, brown eyes, and glasses. They were both our age, and we seemed to know them pretty well in the vision."

The guys all shook their heads. "Never seen them before," Mason said.

"Maybe their names are Parker Thomas and Evelyn Autumn?" Parker said, now standing right behind him.

Mason screamed like a little kid and swatted his hand through the air. I felt a strong gust of wind next to me, and Parker flew into the air and landed right in the middle of the frozen fountain. There was a resounding crack as she fell through the ice.

"AGHH!" she screamed. "THAT'S FREEZING!"

I ran to the edge of the fountain, and she got to her feet, soaked.

"Do you always throw people into fountains?!" she asked, glaring at Mason. "Look at me. I'm soaked! And it's winter!"

"Well, you snuck up on me!" Mason yelled at her.

Good job at introducing ourselves, I thought.

"You should have noticed that I was there! It wasn't like I jumped out and yelled 'boo' as loud as I could! I'm *soaked*!"

Then, a thought occurred to me. "Parker, hold out your hand."

She raised her eyebrows but did it anyway.

I grabbed her hand and concentrated.

Slowly, the water faded away, and Parker was standing there completely dry, like nothing had happened.

"You can dry things off, too?" Parker asked.

"I mean, I can summon water, so it would make sense that I could get rid of it too," I said.

She shrugged, "That makes sense, and thank you." She turned towards Luna. "You had a vision?"

Luna nodded. "Yup. You guys are definitely the other people I saw."

"Wait," the last person, a boy, spoke up. He'd been quiet until now, so I hadn't paid attention to him. He had light blue eyes and blonde hair. He wore a red robe over normal clothing. "We need to introduce ourselves!" He held out his hand. "I'm Austin Hunt, and I'm a Flame, otherwise known as the children of fire."

"Fire, that's cool," I said. "Well, actually, fire isn't cold, but you get my point."

He gave a small laugh. "I got what you mean."

"Wait," Parker asked, "Are your parents Colten and Ellie Hunt?"

He didn't seem surprised by that question. "Yeah, did they help you get to the island?"

I nodded, "Yeah, they did."

He shrugged. "I'm not surprised."

"Anyway," Luna said, "I'm Luna Everett, Speaker."

"I'm Mason Remington, a Windy," Mason said.

"I could tell," Parker said, "as you sent me flying into a frozen fountain on a gust of wind."

"Moving on," said the boy with the white robe, "I'm Daniel Crawford, a Freezer."

"He makes really good snow forts." Luna smiled at him.

He smiled back at her, "And you're great at defending them."

She blushed, and I didn't have to be a genius to know that there was something going on between them.

"My name is Parker Thomas," Parker told them, "and I can control nature with my fellow Forestus, who I have never met."

"And I'm Evelyn Autumn," I said. "I'm an Oceanus."

Luna studied us. "I had a vision about you two last night, and then, today, I meet you. I've never seen you guys here before."

"We just got here today," I told her.

"Well, that makes sense. Speakers are usually shown visions

that are important at the time. It's not always the future, either. Sometimes we are shown visions from the past or things that are happening right now."

"Hold on," Parker said, "two things. First of all, you can see the present, too? And things that happened in the past?"

Luna nodded, "Sure can."

"Second of all, have you ever told a prophecy before? What's it like?"

"No, I . . . I haven't, but some of the others told me that when it happens you still remember doing it, but you can't control what you say or do. It's like someone else is controlling you." She shuddered, "That just makes it sound creepy."

"Maybe it won't happen to you?" I told her.

She shook her head, "It happens at least once to all Speakers. Usually only two or three times, but for some it can happen constantly."

"Feeling like you're being controlled on a daily basis is not my idea of fun," I said.

Everyone agreed.

"So, what was this vision about?" I asked.

"She just started to tell us," Austin said, "but then, as soon as she said we were in it and mentioned a dark hallway, Mason started asking her questions."

"Hey!" Mason retaliated, "I was just being curious."

"Curiosity killed the cat," Parker told him.

"Today's your first day here, and you're walking around without a Leader, which means you're probably exploring. And when you explore, you usually do it out of, guess what, *curiosity*."

I interrupted before a fight could start. "Luna, you were saying?"

"We were in this dark hallway," she said, "and we all had our ears up to this door, clearly listening to something. Suddenly, we jumped away from the door. It banged open, and a Curser jumped out. Evelyn sprayed him with a jet of water, and then, well . . . " She shrugged, "It ended, just like that. I don't know what happened next."

"That was it?" I asked.

She nodded, "Yup."

"Like, nothing else? Not a single thing?"

"Not a single thing," she assured me.

"A dark hallway does not sound fun," Parker said.

I shuddered. This may sound childish, but I'm afraid of the dark. You never know what's there, and that scares me. Something could easily come up behind you and . . .

Nope, not going to think about that.

"It sounds like we were eavesdropping on them," Mason pointed out. "So wherever we are, it's probably their territory."

"Why would we be there?" I wondered aloud.

Luna shook her head, "I have no idea, and I'm confused because we looked the same age we are now, but there's no way they would let any of us out of Enchantia on our own."

I was about to comment, but then—

Dong. Dong. Dong.

It was the sound of a loud bell ringing.

"What's that?" Parker asked.

"One word," Mason said. "Food!"

We walked over to the dining hall, which was a long building with tall windows and filled with round tables to sit at. At each table were eight chairs, eight plates, and eight sets of silverware, as well as salt and pepper shakers.

These people really liked the number eight.

We found a table near a window and sat down.

"Where's the food?" Parker asked.

"Right here." Mason grabbed a plate off the table and said, "Steak!"

Steak appeared on the plate.

"Cool," Parker picked up her plate and thought for a moment. "Chicken taco!"

A chicken taco appeared.

The rest of us ordered our food and drinks (the cups worked the same way) and started talking.

"So where are you guys from?" I asked them.

"Detroit," Austin replied.

"San Francisco," Mason said.

"New York City," Luna told us.

"Phoenix, Arizona," Daniel said.

"You're a freezer from Arizona?" I asked.

"Yeah, kind of weird, isn't it?"

Parker put down her taco, "I'm from Chicago."

"I'm from Ann Arbor," I told them.

Daniel frowned, "Where's that?"

"It's a small town in Michigan," I explained.

"Oh, okay," Austin gave a small grin. "You're a small town girl."

"Livin' in a lonely world!" Mason sang.

I laughed, but, before any of us could continue, a piercing scream came from outside the window.

Everyone in the hall stopped and turned towards the windows on our side of the room.

Since it was winter, the sun was already setting, but I could still see Raven running towards us. Even from inside, we could hear her screaming:

"Attack!" she was yelling. "The Cursers are attacking!"

Behind her, parked at the docks, I saw a big boat. It was one of those pirate-type ships, and a group of people wearing dark robes was standing on the docks next to it.

The Cursers were here.

From their table in the middle of the room, the rest of the Leaders jumped up and ran to the window.

"Impossible!" Mr. Hudson exclaimed. "They can't get in!"

Standing next to him, Ms. Maple shook her head. "Never in history have they gotten on the island. You have to be with someone who has been in before–" she faltered, coming to a realization.

Everyone in the hall started whispering to their friends.

At our table, we all turned and looked at each other.

"A traitor," Luna whispered. "Someone let them in."

"But who?" I asked. "I thought we weren't allowed to leave the island without permission."

"Everyone, listen up!" Mr. Hudson called. "Us Leaders are going after them. Please go immediately to the castle and stay there until further notice. Hurry now!"

You didn't need to tell us twice. Everyone jumped to their feet and bolted for the door.

"They aren't going to hold them off on their own," Daniel said, once we got outside. "There's too many!"

"I'm going to help," said a girl who was walking next to us.

"Same here," said one of the boys.

"Let's go!" someone shouted, and a small group of people

took off towards the shore.

"Should we help?" Mason asked.

Parker looked terrified, but she slowly nodded. "They need all the help they can get."

The six of us started sprinting towards the Cursers, but we barely got anywhere before, out of the corner of my eye, I thought I saw something moving through the shadows of the buildings.

"Guys, stop running!" I yelled.

They turned to face me, and I pointed. "Do you see that?"

All of them looked where I was pointing, and, sure enough, there was a dark figure moving silently across the island.

"Who's that?" Parker asked.

"I don't know," I said, "but I don't like it. They're up to something."

"We should follow them!" Mason said. "See what they're up to!"

"That sounds dangerous," I remarked. "Who knows what they're doing?"

"Then let's find out," Mason said.

"But–" I started.

"You're coming," Parker said with finality.

Mason and Parker took off towards them, and, reluctantly, I followed with everyone else.

Once we got close, we hid in the shadow of one of the buildings and watched.

The Curser was heading towards the doors of the castle. No one was there to protect them. Everyone was either hiding or fighting. They reached the doors, opened them, and slipped inside.

Staying hidden, the six of us made our way to the doors. Once we got to them, we carefully pulled them open and peeked through. Hiding there, we watched the Curser pull open the doors to the library and enter.

We tiptoed across the common area, careful not to make noise, and opened the doors to the library.

The Curser had their back to us, and they were walking back and forth among the shelves, inspecting the books. Every once in a while, they would pull out a book, seemingly at random, and flip through it before putting it back on the shelf.

I took a step forward and yelled, "Hey!"

The Curser turned, but kept their hood pulled down so we couldn't see who they were.

I heard a familiar growl. "What do we have here?"

It was one of the same Cursers from yesterday, the woman who had been looking for me in my school.

"Well, well," she said, "I remember some of you. Autumn, I finally get to show you my tricks. And next to you, the Thomas girl. I remember you and your plants."

Parker glared at her. "Yeah, but I escaped."

"Ah," she said, "but I didn't get to show you what I could do."

She spread her arms, and the temperature in the room dropped to freezing. The roaring fire died completely, leaving no trace that it had been there. Behind us, the door slammed shut.

I instinctively turned around, grabbed a handle, and pulled. It didn't budge.

We were trapped.

The Curser laughed. "I went easy on you last time. I let you escape, so that I could capture you all at once. But now, you will have no choice but to come with me to our base in the mountains. There's nothing to do but sit here and wait."

Then, I heard someone knock a rhythm on the door:

Knock. Pause. *Knock, knock.* Pause. *Knock.*

The door opened, and five more Cursers walked in. Unlike the others I had seen, their hoods were down so I could see their faces.

"Excellent!" she said. "Enchanters, hands behind your backs please."

We reluctantly obeyed.

Each of the Cursers walked forward and grabbed one of our hands, keeping them behind our backs.

Surprisingly, the woman walked forward and grabbed mine.

"Don't you think about doing anything," she whispered in my ear. "If you interfere, one of them gets hurt. Understand?"

I nodded slowly, confused as to why, out of everyone, she had gone after me. "I understand."

"Good."

"Hey!" Austin raised his eyebrows at her. "Are you threatening Evelyn?"

"Not at all," she lied.

"Don't . . . don't you dare think about hurting any of them," he said, "or I'll . . . I'll . . . "

"Nice try, but it's a little too late," she said and kicked me, hard, in the ankle.

"Ouch!" I yelped.

"I said don't!"

"AGGHH!" Austin's captor let go of his hands, and I saw that the Curser's hands were blackened and burnt.

Mason yelled, and a gust of wind blew the rest of the Cursers off their feet.

We ran out the door, not once looking back.

CHAPTER 7

LUNA TELLS US SECRETS

We bolted across the central green, heading towards a mixed group of people rushing around. The air was filled with smoke and bursts of bright light, signs of the small battle between the Cursers and Enchanters. It was terrifying. All I could see was blurred shapes moving around.

Someone in a teal robe ran out of the chaos and rushed over to us. As he got closer, I realized who it was.

"You!" The look on Mr. Hudson's face was of pure anger. "You did this!"

"I did what?" I asked, confused.

"You let them in, didn't you?! They had never been able to get in before you showed up! Don't think for one second that you won't pay!" He raised his hands, palms facing us.

I closed my eyes instinctively, preparing for whatever it was that Mr. Hudson would no doubt do. But then, a piercing scream split through the sky.

"Amelia!" I heard Mr. Hudson scream.

I opened my eyes. He had apparently forgotten about us and

was now running back towards the crowd of people fighting.

Someone grabbed my arm. "Let's go!" Austin shouted.

I turned, and, together, we ran a different way towards the stables. We reached them and ran inside. For a second, no one said anything.

"This is bad," Luna said. "They think *we* let the Cursers in?"

"Not going to lie," Parker said, "I can kind of see where he's coming from."

"You didn't, did you?" Mason raised his eyebrows at Parker.

"Of course not! You think I could even do something like that? You threw me in a freaking fountain like it was nothing for crying out loud!"

"Guys!" Daniel yelled. "Can you both please stop for a minute?"

Everyone was quiet as Daniel asked, "What are we going to do now?"

After another minute of silence, I spoke up. "Run."

Everybody stared at me in shock, but I just shrugged. "What else are we going to do? We're wanted on both sides. Do we really have a choice?"

Mason looked like he might say something, but Parker talked before he could. "We could ride the pegasi away from here." She pointed around at all the winged horses in the stables. "But we have no supplies," Mason pointed out.

"I still have my bag in my room," Parker said. "We can fly up to my window, and I can go in and get it."

"We could get plates and cups from the kitchen," Austin said, "so that way we don't have to rely on just fruits and vegetables. No offense, Parker."

"None taken."

"I'll go with you to get those," I told Austin. "If you need to use your powers at all, the best person you can have with you is someone who can control water."

"I can go with Parker," Mason said, "make sure she doesn't fall while trying to climb in her window."

"So now you think I'm going to fall?"

"It's just a precaution!"

"What are Luna and I supposed to do?" Daniel said.

"You guys can come with me and Parker," Mason said.

Luna walked up to a pegasus with a dark purple coat. "This is my horse, Legend. She's a wonderful flier. I can ride on her with Daniel."

"We can take Storm," Mason told Parker, petting a white pegasus with splashes of gray on him.

I looked at Austin. "Who should we take?"

He smiled. "I know."

I followed him over to a pegasus with a light brown coat and golden mane.

"Who's this?" I asked.

"This is Aqua," he said. "She's a water horse and can fly in both water and the air. She doesn't have an owner. She's a free spirit. I think you'll get along."

I reach up to rub her. "She's beautiful."

Just then, I heard someone approaching outside.

"Guys," Luna whispered, "let's go!"

We flew above the stables, and I looked down to see the Cursers standing in front of them. Their mouths were hanging wide open in awe.

Storm and Legend went towards the castle, while Aqua, carrying me and Austin, flew towards the kitchen.

She set us down outside the door, and Austin ran in and grabbed two plates and two cups. (We could share: The plates gave out an unlimited amount of food.) Then we took off into the sky, going back the way we came.

We met back up with everyone else directly above the stables and, together, soared away from Enchantia, watching as it slowly faded away into the horizon.

I couldn't resist giving a little sigh. "Seriously?" I muttered.

"What?" Austin asked.

"I didn't even get a day here. I never got to use the pool or the library or even try out the bed in my room."

"Don't say that. You will get time here. It's not like we're escaping forever."

"How can you say that? I've never had a home that actually feels like home!" I spat out without thinking. "Imagine living your whole life alone, then being given a fresh start, and having it get taken away from you before you even had a chance at it!" I stopped and blushed, realizing that I had said way too much.

He shook his head. "You *are* getting a fresh start. But part of starting over is that it isn't easy. It's hard, it's difficult, and it takes time. But, in the end, it will be the best thing that ever happened to you. Trust me."

That was saying a lot. I had just met him. He didn't know me. He didn't know what I'd been through.

But, surprisingly, I found I could trust him, if only for the moment.

Just then, Parker and Mason pulled up to us in the air. "Where should we go?" Parker asked.

"I have no idea," I replied.

"How about we talk with Luna and Daniel and then decide?" Austin asked.

Mason shook his head, "Can't do that."

Austin frowned. "How come?"

Both of them pointed down, and we looked and saw that both Luna and Daniel had fallen asleep on Legend.

"That's why not," Parker said.

"They fell asleep quickly," I remarked.

"Well," Austin said, "they were both up late last night doing schoolwork. They've been pretty tired all day."

"Anyway, with the question of where we should go, if we want to go with what Luna said earlier, a dark hallway," Mason said. "But, if I could choose, I'd go somewhere tropical."

"If we keep going this way, we will end up somewhere tropical," Austin pointed out. "We're heading south."

"Wait, we are?" I asked.

He nodded, "The stables are on the south side of the island, because the castle faces west. So if we continue this way, then we'll most likely end up in the Gulf of Mexico."

"Oooo," I said, excited. "I love the ocean!"

"You're an *Oceanus*," Mason pointed out. "You can *control water*. I'd be more surprised if you said you hated the ocean."

I shrugged, "I guess you're right."

Parker, Mason, and Austin talked a little more about where we might go, and I looked to my right at the sunset.

It was beautiful tonight. I could see many different shades of red, orange, and yellow all coming together in one giant piece of art.

Then, on the horizon, I spotted a gray outline.

"Guys, look," I said, pointing.

As we flew closer, I could make out a long cliff jutting out over the huge lake. I saw snowy trees perched on top of all the rock.

"Land there," I demanded.

Aqua, Legend, and Storm landed softly on the snow, barely making a sound.

Still on Legend, Luna and Daniel groaned and opened their eyes.

"Where are we?" Luna asked.

"On a cliff," Mason said, in the same tone you would use to talk about the weather. "We can stay here tonight."

"Okay, good," Daniel said, which was not a person's usual reaction when someone tells you you're on a cliff. "I'm tired."

"You were *just* sleeping," Parker pointed out.

"Well, I'm still tired."

We got off the horses and found some sticks and rocks, so we made a fire pit, and Austin started a bonfire. (I may or may not have grinned and said, *"Ooo! Fire!"* There is nothing wrong with me.)

"Marshmallows!" Mason exclaimed, holding up one of the plates.

We all laughed and grabbed a marshmallow off the plate. Using some long sticks we found, we decided to roast them. The pegasi sat down near the edge of the clearing, and we sat down to talk.

"So," Luna started, "how did you escape the Cursers? The first time, we know the second."

I told them about all that had happened. As I talked, I started to relax. I hadn't even noticed how tense I'd been. Storytelling was something I loved to do, and, as I told my story, I kinda forgot that they were there. When I was done, I looked up to see them all still staring at me.

"That's what happened," I finished.

"That's a lot to happen in two days," Mason said.

"Yeah, it is," I agreed.

"Do you think your parents are worried?" Daniel asked.

"You mean about the fact their only child went missing? Yeah, probably."

"I haven't seen my parents in a week," Parker said.

"I haven't seen my parents in years," Mason muttered.

Parker raised her eyebrows at him. "How come?"

He sighed. "I'm an orphan."

Parker's expression turned sad. "Did you know them?"

He nodded, and a single tear flowed down his cheek. "I was six and at daycare when they got into a car crash. I didn't have any other living family members."

A few tears formed in Parker's eyes. "I'm sorry I asked about it."

"It's fine. I was going to have to tell someday," Mason said.

Then Parker did something that surprised all of us: She scooted over and gave Mason a hug.

"I would say I'm sorry," she told him, "but that won't cover it."

"It can't bring them back," he agreed. "I've gone to many different foster homes the past few years, but none of them lasted. Not too long ago, I ran away. Eventually, I found Enchantia, and I've stayed there ever since."

Luna shook her head. "Listen, Mason, I—" She froze and stood up with a dazed expression.

A little ways away, the horses whinnied nervously.

Daniel looked worried, "Luna?"

Luna stared off into space for a second and then started reciting:

"Six Enchanters shall fly in the sky
To catch a traitor in her lie.
Fire and water combined pursue
And start a quest to find the two."

Luna finished and sat back down. The dazed expression faded from her face. We all stared at her in stunned silence.

Finally, Mason spoke up. "I don't think that was what you meant to say."

She shook her head, "Not at all."

Daniel stated the obvious. "Your first prophecy."

"Yeah," she said, stunned. "It was just like they'd described. I had no control, but I remember everything."

"'*Six Enchanters shall fly in the sky*,'" I murmured, "'*To catch a traitor in her lie.*' The Enchanters are obviously us."

"Well no kidding," Parker said.

"'*Fire and water combined pursue*,'" Mason recited.

Everyone looked at me and Austin.

"What are we pursuing?" he wondered aloud, looking at me.

I shook my head. "No idea."

"'*And start a quest to find the two*,'" Parker finished, "The two what? That line makes no sense!"

"None," Daniel agreed.

"So what do we do?" I asked.

"Nothing right now," Luna said. "We just have to wait."

"But I can't wait!" I exclaimed. "I'm incredibly impatient!"

"Then you'll have to work on that," Parker said.

Mason stood up and stretched. I could see in his eyes that he was still upset after talking about his parents. "I don't know about you, but I'm tired. Let's talk in the morning."

We decided to sleep in shifts, with Parker and I for first watch, Daniel and Luna for second, and Mason and Austin for third.

I talked to Parker about my life in Michigan, and she told me about Chicago. She told me that she had four siblings: an older brother and sister and a younger brother and sister. I liked Parker. She seemed to be a fun person.

We talked for a few hours before waking up Luna and Daniel for their watch. When I lay down in the snow to go to sleep, the last thing I thought was that maybe, just maybe, I might be able to make some new friends.

Which was weird, because I'd given up on that a long time ago.

CHAPTER 8

THEY FOLLOWED US

We packed up early the next morning and took off, each of us riding the same pegasus as yesterday. Until we figured out what to do next, our only goal was to get as far away as possible from Enchantia and the Cursers.

Austin, who had third watch last night, was asleep behind me, but I didn't mind. After flying for a little while, he started snoring.

I'll admit, I thought it was pretty cute.

Legend and Storm pulled up next to me in the air.

Apparently, Austin was not the only one tired out. Mason was also asleep behind Parker.

"I think they're tired," Parker said.

"Just a little bit," I agreed sarcastically.

Luna looked down at the snowy fields that had replaced the water. "Is Ohio all cornfields?"

"Pretty much," I said.

"Where do we even go from here?" Luna asked. "We ran away during the attack. That looks really bad."

"I have no idea," Daniel said, "but it better have soft beds and warm showers."

"It's kind of hard to find soft beds and warm showers while you're on the run," Parker pointed out. "It's not like you're going to find that in the middle of the snow."

"How about we just keep flying south and see if we can find anything?" I suggested.

"I'm good with that," Parker said, "but we *will* have to go back."

"True," I agreed, "Just not yet. We don't know what happened after we left."

"What's that?" Luna asked, alarmed and pointing down.

I looked where she was pointing. There was a small road right underneath us, but no cars were on it. Instead, I could see three figures in dark robes standing in the middle of the street, looking up at us. I realized right away who it was and said a few words in my head that I would never say aloud.

"Cursers," Luna shook her head, "Not good."

"We're going to have to talk to them, aren't we?" Parker asked, fear in her eyes.

Luna nodded. "Afraid so."

Parker turned around on Storm to face Mason. She shook him violently. "Wake up! We have company!"

"Austin, wake up," I turned and tapped Austin on the

shoulder a few times.

They both groaned and opened their eyes.

"What time is it?" Mason yawned.

"Time to wake up," Parker replied.

"Cursers?" Austin asked sleepily.

"That's what we think," I told him.

We directed the pegasi towards the ground. I couldn't read the expression on their faces, but they were definitely not surprised to see us. We landed in the middle of the road, facing them. None of us dismounted. We never knew when we would need a quick get away.

"Okay," Parker started. "I'm going to get straight to the point. You guys are Cursers trying to kidnap us. But we don't want that, so we're just going to try to run away now. However, you aren't going to let us get away, and you're going to chase or fight us. Did I miss anything?" She glanced around at all of us.

One of them, a guy, laughed. "Well, it seems like you're a fast learner. My name's Casper, and I am a Curser. However, I actually do have something to add."

"What?" Parker challenged.

"I will admit that I like your attitude. You've got courage, girly. I'm here to make you an offer."

Parker snorted. "An offer? From you? Do you think I've lost my mind?"

"Join us, and you will get him back. He's alive, Parker."

She looked like she had taken a punch to the face. I had no clue what was going on, but I figured it had something to do with why she had run away.

Whatever the offer was, it must have been a big deal to her.

"Parker," I whispered, "don't listen to them."

She suddenly sat up straight and glared at Casper. "I never would. You're a liar, Casper. You wouldn't give him back. I'm an Enchanter. I'm staying on this side."

He shrugged. "It was worth a try. You can stay with them, but one day you will regret your decision. With us, you could live a long life. You could be powerful, rich, and famous! Instead of experiencing heartbreak and losing. The Enchanters will lose, and you'll go down with them. Our Speakers have guaranteed this. You just wait, girly. Someday, you will wish you came when you had the chance."

"I will never regret staying over here," Parker retaliated, but I could hear a tint of fear in her voice that perfectly matched the look in her eyes. "This is where I belong."

"Then fine, I guess I have no choice but to do the alternative," he said. "Prisoners it is."

"No way!" I yelled, and Aqua took off into the sky with Legend and Storm.

One of the Cursers shot a ball of fire up at Aqua, and I blasted it out of the air with water.

Another shot a huge snowball (when I say huge, I mean it was actually six feet tall) straight towards Legend. Daniel knocked it out of the air with his own giant snowball.

The last one, Casper, waved his arm and a giant tree popped up in the middle of the road: directly in the path of Storm and his riders.

The pegasus tried to swerve, but it was too close. He slammed into the side of the tree, and the three of them fell towards the ground. Just before they made contact, Mason screamed. They suddenly stopped and slowly floated down the last couple feet.

Parker and Mason quickly got to their feet, but Storm stayed on the ground. One of his wings was bent, but, luckily, I could see that his eyes were open and moving, so at least he wasn't dead.

Casper laughed. "I was a Forestus too, Parker. I left the Enchanters to come join the better side."

Parker glared at him. "All I'm hearing is that you are a traitor, and the fact that your side is full of those does not make it sound like the winning side."

"Well, you see," he explained, "the winning side is the one who beats the other. Seeing as your horse is in no condition to fly, you have nowhere to run away. So you have two options: one, surrender and come peacefully. Or two, try to fight us and lose."

"How about option three?" I asked, landing Aqua next to Parker.

"Yeah!" Mason nodded, "You see, you think options one or two are amazing, but I'm sad to inform you that I'm not a fan. So we'll create our own option."

"And what is it?" Casper asked.

"This," Mason grinned wickedly, and the Curser flew up twenty feet into the air and started falling back down towards the earth. A five foot tall pile of leaves appeared underneath him, and he crashed into it. When he stood up, I was surprised to see that he wasn't hurt. Normal leaves don't do that much for protection. Trust me, I know. Falling into a leaf pile is fun until you fall the wrong way.

(Quick life lesson: You can get hurt doing anything.)

"You think a little wind could hurt me?" he sneered, "Got to try better than that."

"Why don't you fight us instead of resisting?" Parker taunted. "Are you scared?"

He smiled, and I was so scared about what it meant I had to resist the urge to run away and hide in a hole. "No, but using too much power at once will drain you. I want to see what you can handle doing before you're too weak to fight. And there is no harm in telling you this because the alternative for using your powers is waiting for my backup to come and outnumber you."

Daniel and Luna flew down next to us, and the other two Cursers, who had been pelting them with fireballs and snowballs, came over and stood next to Casper.

"So basically," I summed up, "you're too much of a coward to fight us?"

He glared at me. "I'm not a coward."

"Oh, really?" Parker scratched her chin, "Because you're scared to fight people with almost no magic experience? Totally not a coward."

"I'll show you a coward!"

Parker looked at me and mouthed, *Distract him.*

I relayed this to Austin.

"We can do that," he whispered.

I leaned next to Aqua's ear. "We need to cause a disturbance. Can you–"

She neighed like she understood, and took off into the air.

All three Cursers laughed and shook their heads.

"Talk about cowards!" The one on the right said. "They're running away and leaving their friends as bait!"

That's what you think, I thought.

Thirty feet above the ground, Aqua stopped, flipped over in mid-air, and dove straight down towards the ground: straight towards the three Cursers waiting there.

Three pairs of eyes grew wide, and they ran back in alarm.

However, we weren't trying to actually hit them. We were just trying to make them think we were.

Aqua swooped less than a foot over their heads, and Austin shot a fireball towards them. One of them shot their own fireball, and the two balls of fire collided in the air. It was like watching a small meteorite explode.

I looked down at the snow, knowing that it was really just frozen water. I could use that to my advantage.

I waved my arm, and a small geyser erupted in the middle of the snowy plain. That made me question:

What else could I do?

"Aqua!" I said, "Put me down there! Right in front of the Cursers!"

"What are you doing?" Austin asked in alarm.

"I have no idea!"

Aqua flew low in between our friends and the Cursers, and I jumped off and landed on my feet.

I kinda scared myself. I could jump off a flying pegasus, stick the landing, and challenge a few people in dark robes, but I couldn't remember to set my own alarm in the morning?

Yes, people, that's me.

I faced them and they laughed.

"The waterling has come to play!" The one on the left, this one a girl, cackled. "You want to have a water fight?"

I grinned at them. "I sure do."

I raised my arms, and two geysers, one on each side of me, shot up into the air.

"You want a water fight? You got one." I told them.

I looked Casper straight in the eye and yelled at the top of my lungs.

A giant wave of water burst out of the cement in front of me and knocked into them, sending them flying across the pavement.

Another simple wave of my hand and a geyser shot up underneath them. They soared into the sky, screaming like they were falling off a cliff, even though they were pretty much doing the opposite. I ran back towards my friends.

Aqua had landed back on the ground next to everyone else, and Austin was kneeling next to Storm.

"What should we do?" I asked them.

Parker raised her eyebrows at me. "Showoff."

"I'm not a showoff."

"You just made three Cursers soar into the sky on a geyser, and you're not even a little tired," she pointed out. "Showoff."

"Well," I said, "on other topics, we need to go! I only delayed them–"

Suddenly, I heard a *thunk* from behind me and turned around to see a mountain of snow, which all three Cursers were standing on.

The girl glared at me. "You little—"

I will not say what word she used to describe me. Trust me, it's a bad one.

"Watch your language!" I glared at her, "Unless you really like geysers."

"You think your little jokes are so funny," Casper said, "but soon, we'll be the ones telling the jokes."

"Really?" I jerked my hand upward, and another geyser shot them back up into the air.

"Not going to lie," I admitted, "that's kind of fun."

Parker looked at me. "Storm needs help. We need to get her to a Healer."

Mason, sitting on the ground next to Austin, shook his head. He looked really worried. "None of us are Healers. We have water, fire, air, nature, prophecy, and snow. No healing."

Then, an idea came to me. "Guys, I think I may know where to go, but it's a little far. I don't think we would be able to get there with one pegasus down."

"Where?" Mason asked, and he started talking at a mile a minute. "I don't care if it's on the other side of the country, I will get us there."

I raised my eyebrows at him, "Can you get us to my house in Michigan?"

"I could do that," he said.

"But how?" Parker asked, "Mason, what are you thinking?"

He smiled at her. "You'll see, but I may also need a Healer afterwards. It's quite a bit of magic."

Parker looked scared. "*Mason Remington, please* tell me what you're planning."

"Don't worry about me, Parks. I'll be fine."

I described where I lived to Mason, and then I heard another *thud* from behind me. All of us turned around to see the Cursers making their way towards us.

"Ugh!" Casper glared at me, "If you do that one more time–"

"What?" I demanded, and put my hands on my hips. "What are you gonna do?"

(Quick life lesson number two: Never say that unless you wish to get in serious trouble.)

Whoosh! Something grabbed my foot, and I shot upwards.

"Ahh!" I screamed, hanging upside down by my ankle. I looked up and saw that a vine hanging from the tree was wrapped around it.

"Put me down!" I yelled.

Austin shot a fireball at the middle of the vine and it passed clean through. I fell, hard, onto the pavement with my arm tucked under me and heard a small crack as my right wrist filled with white-hot pain.

For a second, everything went black. Once I regained a blurry outline of the world, I saw someone run towards me and help me sit up.

Through the haze of pain, I looked up and saw Austin's worried face.

"No, no, no," he whispered. "Evelyn? Are you okay? Did you hit your head?"

"No," I whispered back, "It's my wrist."

He looked down and gasped. "That's definitely broken."

I looked down and tried hard not to faint.

My wrist was bent at an awkward angle, and, already, it was starting to swell. I felt really queasy all of a sudden.

"Now we have two broken people," he muttered.

"No," I corrected, "One broken person and one broken horse."

"Hey!" I looked up to see a blurred Mason glaring at Casper. "That's two: two of my friends you have hurt today. Now no more!"

He snapped his fingers (Which is something I unfortunately can't do, even when my wrist isn't broken.), and all three Cursers fell to the ground like someone invisible had punched them in the face.

Behind him, Parker waved her hand and the huge tree disappeared. She nodded to him, and he raised his arms.

"Good bye, Cursers!" He yelled and threw his arms forward.

The last thing I remembered before passing out was shooting backwards and up, and then starting to quickly descend towards the ground.

CHAPTER 9

I RUN INTO MY PARENTS

The first thing I realized when I woke up was that I was back in my own bed.

That was a weird dream, I thought.

Except for the fact that my wrist hurt . . .

Wait a minute.

I opened my eyes to see a pair of familiar, light blue worried ones looking back at me.

"I'm so sorry," Austin said, "I feel like this is my fault."

I looked at my wrist, which was wrapped up in bandages. The image of it broken popped into my mind, and I quickly pushed the thought away. I didn't need to throw up at that moment. With my good hand, I reached across the bed and grabbed one of Austin's.

"Austin, this isn't your fault. You were trying to save me. I should really thank you. If you hadn't gotten me down, I probably would still be hanging upside down from a vine."

He gave me a tiny smile and squeezed my hand. "How does it feel?"

I shrugged, "It still hurts, but it's definitely better."

I let go of his hand and carefully sat up.

"Where's everyone else?" I asked.

"Luna and Daniel are downstairs talking. Parker is in the guest bedroom with Mason. She'll be happy to know you're awake. Your mom is in there with them. The pegasi are in your backyard, and I'm right here, talking to you."

Then, something dawned on me. "Austin, how long was I out?"

"Only an hour. The rest of us were out for a half hour, with the exception of Mason. He's still passed out."

The door creaked open and my mom walked in. She stopped when she saw that I was awake.

"Evelyn!" Her eyes filled with tears, and she ran forward and hugged me. When she let go, she looked me in the eye. "Evelyn Irene, you scared me to death! Don't you dare do that again!"

"I'm sorry," I told her. "I had no choice."

She nodded and hugged me again. "I understand, but you still scared me and your father. And then I hear that Enchantia was invaded the day after you went missing!" She pointed at Austin. "He explained everything to me. I would have told you, but they made that law years ago that you couldn't tell your children until their thirteenth birthday. So you would have found out soon anyway."

She still had tons of tears in her eyes. I must have really upset her. I'd never seen her that emotional.

She grabbed a tissue from a box on my nightstand and blew her nose. "Sorry, sorry, in other news, the pegasus, Storm, is going to be fine. With my magic, he should be better in two or three days, same with your wrist. Mason just needs rest. He overdid himself with that flying. But . . . how did you know that I was a Healer? You didn't even know that I had powers."

I smiled. "It wasn't that hard to figure out."

All my life, whenever I'd get hurt or sick, my mom always helped me get better almost overnight. When I asked her what it was, she would just tell me, "It's magic, Evelyn." Now, when I found out about the eight Enchanter powers, it was pretty easy to see what hers were. She was known for taking care of people. That was her thing. She was definitely a Healer.

She slowly stood up. "I have to go check on Mason now, but I'll come back in a little bit to check on you again."

She turned and walked out of the room.

Austin watched her walk out and then picked up one of the pictures on my nightstand. "Hey, Evelyn?"

"Yeah?" I asked cautiously.

He turned the picture around. "What's this from?"

I looked at it and recognised it right away.

"Um . . . that's me and my parents . . . at an autism walk."

He raised his eyebrows at me. "There are three people in this picture, your parents and you. Are you autistic?"

I was shocked. I didn't like talking about my autism to other people, but I didn't like lying either. And, since he had directly asked, I couldn't exactly ignore the question.

"Uh-um . . . yeah, I am."

"Do you not like talking about it?"

Once again, I was super surprised. How had he possibly known?

"Yeah," I said, "so please, *please* don't tell anybody else about it."

He nodded, "If you don't want me to tell them, then I won't."

My mom appeared in the doorway.

"Mason's still asleep, but do you guys want to come visit him?"

"Yeah, sure," I replied.

I slowly got out of bed, and we walked across the hall to the guest bedroom. Surprisingly, I had no trouble walking around, even though I had just passed out.

I was greeted by Parker, who yelled, "Evelyn!" and ran to the doorway to give me a bear hug.

"Hey, Parker," I said. "How's Mason?"

"He's fine," she sighed, "but I should have done more! I just let him do that! Maybe there was something I could've done to prevent him from overdoing himself?"

I shook my head. "You guys beat yourself up too much. Everyone's fine! We're alive, and there are no Cursers with us. You did just fine. And everyone gets hurt once in a while!"

Over on the bed, Mason groaned and rolled over in his sleep.

"See that!" I said, "He just said he agrees with me."

Parker shook her head. "He did not. You're making stuff up."

"Maybe I did, maybe I didn't."

"Anyway," my mom interrupted, "you guys are going to have to stay here for a few days."

All three of us looked at Mason on the bed and nodded.

"I think that's a good idea," Parker said.

"I think it is too," she replied. "The girls can stay in Evelyn's room, and the boys can stay in the guest bedroom."

"Okay," I agreed, "and then, Mom, once we're all good to go, we need to go back out."

She stared at me like I had said: *We need to do homework because we love it*!

While I was asleep, something had clicked in my brain.

The second Parker and I arrived at Enchantia, it was attacked for the first time ever. We knew for sure that at least one of the Leaders thought that we let in the Cursers, which meant that we wouldn't be welcomed back until we could prove that we were innocent.

What better way to prove that than by catching the traitor?

I know what you're thinking. *Evelyn, you weren't even at Enchantia for a day, why do you care so much?*

Well, I was always an outsider at my school, and, for the very, *very* short time that I was there, I could see myself having a home. And the Enchanters were such nice people, I thought I could have a place with them.

"Evelyn, listen," Mom said, "I completely trust you, but you can't do that. The Cursers are searching everywhere for you. If they found you–" She shook her head. "As your mom, I have to stop you from doing this. You can stay here, and–"

"No," I argued, "as my mom, you have to let me do this, okay? I will do what I need to do and return to Enchantia. You can visit me on the weekends, and I'll come back in the summer. But this is my one chance to do something great, to find a place where I can *belong*. *Please* let me do this."

She considered it for a minute. I got really worried. *What if she doesn't let me go?* Only after an eternity had passed, she sighed. "Fine, but at least let me help you pack what you need."

I nodded, completely relieved. "Yeah, you can do that. And I'll still need your help. With Mason and Storm in the condition they're in, we're going to be here for a few days."

"Then come downstairs," she said. "Mason needs some time to rest alone."

We walked out of the door and down the stairs into the living room, where my dad was sitting on the couch talking to Luna and Daniel.

He looked up and smiled when we walked in. "Evelyn!" He stood up and gave me a hug. Apparently, everyone wanted hugs today. That was fine by me as I love hugs. "Don't you dare do that again."

"I won't," I promised.

We let go, and he looked around at everyone. "I like them," he whispered, "I'm glad to see you made some new friends."

I smiled. "I am too."

Luna looked up at us. "I just thought of something. What day is it today?"

"December second," my mom replied. "How come?"

Luna's eyes grew big. "Today's my thirteenth birthday."

"Well, then," I said, "should we explain to you that you have magic powers?"

She gave an awkward laugh. "I just thought about it. When we woke up this morning, I forgot what day it was."

Daniel smiled at her. "Well, then, happy birthday! I'm sorry that I didn't get you a present. Actually, I did, but it's back in my room. I'll give it to you whenever we get back to Enchantia."

She smiled back at him. "It's okay. I guess the real present is the fact that we escaped the Cursers. I can probably say that this is going to be the strangest birthday I've ever had, though."

My dad looked at Daniel. "I need to get something from the kitchen. Can you come help me?"

Daniel stood up and gave a crooked grin, "Sure." They both walked out of the living room and through the kitchen door. When they came back, Daniel was holding a square box.

He walked to Luna, and handed her the box.

"What's this?" she asked.

"Open it," he replied.

She opened the lid. "Where'd you get this?"

Inside the box was a round cake with lilac-colored icing. In dark blue letters were the words *Happy Birthday, Luna*!

"I was the first one awake after we all passed out," he explained, "and I remembered that it was your birthday. So I asked Mr. Autumn if I could borrow his kitchen to make a cake. Luckily, he had some purple dye and vanilla frosting so that I could make it your favorite color. Do you like it?"

Luna looked like she was about to start crying. "I love it."

Suddenly, I heard someone say, "Are you guys eating cake without me?"

I turned towards the door of the living room where Mason was standing with his arms crossed.

"How dare you eat dessert without me here! Especially after I just saved your lives."

"That was very risky, Mason Remington!" Parker glared at him, "You could've been killed."

"It was that or be cornered by Cursers. I decided to at least try. And, hey, it worked!"

"That was still a very big risk you took. You need to stay here and rest. No more flying for a few days, okay?"

He gave a small grin. "Yeah, I'll rest."

"Good."

Mason walked over and plopped down on the couch. "It's cake time."

"And talk time," Luna said, "We need a plan."

"But it's your birthday," Daniel said.

"But it's time to make a plan."

"Well," I started, "we need to figure out who let the Cursers into Enchantia. Someone had to let them in."

Parker looked deep in thought. "But Casper said that he used to be an Enchanter. If I'm getting this right, that means he should just be able to get in himself."

"That's where the boundary gets made between the Enchanters and the Cursers," Luna explained. "As long as everyone considers you to be an Enchanter, you're an Enchanter, and the magic works the normal way. But the second everyone finds out that you're actually working for the Cursers, that's when it gets complicated. Once you're a known Curser, you get locked out unless someone still thought of as an Enchanter lets you in."

For a minute, we were in stunned silence. Then, Daniel shook his head. "Every day you surprise me more and more."

"That's complicated," I said, "but it doesn't give us a plan."

"And we're doomed." Mason said.

"We need to be positive," Luna said, "Does anyone have any idea who it might be?"

For a full minute, nobody answered. Then Parker sighed, "I actually might know where we could get some clues to that."

"Where?" I asked.

"My own home," she said, "in Chicago, Illinois."

CHAPTER 10

PARKER FINDS THE RUINS

We spent the next two days resting at my house, deciding what we needed to bring.

I emptied out my school backpack and filled it with all the supplies we could possibly need, as well as a pencil and a small, empty notebook I had found in my bedroom. I had decided to keep a journal of all our adventures. Not for any particular reason, I just did.

Parker still wouldn't say why she wanted to go back to her home, and, anytime any of us tried asking her, she would just respond: "You'll see." We would stop when we saw the sad look in her eyes.

I'll admit, it really worried me. What was so bad that she couldn't tell us about it?

I had just finished packing when I heard a noise and looked up to see Parker standing in the doorway with her bag slung over her back.

"You ready?" she asked.

I slung my own backpack over my coat (My *own* coat: I no

longer needed to use the old one from the janitor's closet.) and looked around at the bright walls of my bedroom.

It occurred to me that if things didn't go well, this may very well be the last time I was here. I had spent my entire life waking up here to do the same school routine every day. Now, I was going on an adventure to help out a magical school. I didn't even know where I would wake up tomorrow.

It's amazing how things can change so fast.

But, I actually *liked* this change.

I nodded, "Yeah, I am."

We walked downstairs to find everyone waiting at the front door.

"Please stay safe," Mom said, giving me a hug, "and remember that we always love you."

My dad also gave me a hug, and told me to be careful. Next thing I knew, we were walking out the front door to where the pegasi were waiting, all of them ready to go.

I mounted Aqua with Austin, and we took off, watching the ground get smaller and smaller.

"To Chicago!" Mason shouted.

As we flew over cornfields, I brought out the notebook and wrote down what had happened to us in the past few days.

When I was done, I looked behind me at Austin, who had been reading over my shoulder as I wrote.

He smiled. "I hope that notebook is big enough."

"Me too."

I looked down at the giant lake underneath us. We were flying over the very tip of Lake Michigan, and soon I would finally figure out what had happened to Parker before I met her in the woods.

I'll admit, there was a tiny part of my brain that couldn't help but think: *What if* she *was the traitor*? What if, right then, she was leading us into a trap, and that was why she wouldn't talk about her reasons?

"Guys, look!" Luna shouted.

I looked forward and watched as the gloomy outlines of buildings grew bigger and bigger. It was really cloudy that day, which just reinforced my feeling that something bad was about to happen.

But apparently nothing could ruin Mason's mood because he just pointed straight ahead and yelled, "Land ahoy!"

Parker shook her head. "We're not pirates."

"I can be whatever I want," Mason retaliated.

We reached the city and flew between the tall buildings. I knew none of the people in the city could see us, but I still wondered how that was possible. All these people, and none of them noticed we were flying pegasi through the sky?

We flew down low and continued, Storm in the lead. Parker

seemed to know where she was going, which was really good because I knew if I was in there by myself I would have been completely lost.

Eventually, we turned into a side street that I wouldn't have seen if Parker hadn't led us into it. The first thing I noticed was the fact that this street was empty: no cars, no people, no nothing, just tall, empty apartments. There were cobwebs in every corner, dust on the windowsills, and a layer of grime and dirt over everything. It seemed like no one had lived there for years.

I didn't need to be a Speaker to know that the place had a history of trouble.

We landed in the middle of the road, and Parker hopped off first. She looked around with a dazed expression on her face.

"It's . . . it's empty," she stuttered. "Why . . . why is it empty?"

Her eyes locked on the door of one of the apartment buildings, and, suddenly, she started sprinting towards it.

"Parker!" I practically jumped off Aqua and hurried after her with everyone else behind me.

She flung open the door and ran inside.

"Parker! Wait up!" I called.

I chased her down a hallway filled with cobwebs, trying not to look at them. I knew if I saw a spider I would scream and run as fast as possible in the other direction. When we reached a staircase, she bolted up it. I, however, tripped on the first step and fell face-first into the stairs.

"Ouch!" I looked up to see her still going. I quickly got to my feet and continued following her. One floor, two floors, eventually she stopped on the landing of the sixth floor.

"Parker Thomas!" I yelled at her, "What was that about?"

She pointed to one of the doors, number 603. "That's my apartment, Evelyn. This is where I grew up. This is where the Cursers came after me."

I took a step forward, "Explain. What happened?"

She sighed, "Evelyn—"

"Tell me," I insisted.

She took a shuddering breath. "It was about two weeks ago. I'd just gotten home from school, and everything seemed . . . normal. The building was the same it had always been. Dad was at home, but my mom was at work. My little siblings were at school. I heard a knock on our front door. My . . . dad went to open it, and there was a Curser standing outside it. She . . . she told him to turn over his Forestus daughter."

"You," Daniel said as he appeared at the top of the staircase along with everyone else. "She wanted you."

Parker nodded. "When he refused to hand me over, she came in, followed by four others. She told me to come with her. Dad locked eyes with me and told me to run. So I ran to the fire escape and climbed down. I could hear a fight going on in the apartment behind me. I wanted to help, but I knew interfering could just make things worse. When I got to the bottom, I heard someone behind me and looked up to see her on the balcony. D-dad . . . my dad . . . was nowhere to be seen."

I felt a tear fall down my cheek, but I didn't say anything.

Parker continued. "I was so angry, I didn't even know what I was doing. I did this weird wave with my hand, and a giant tree appeared in the middle of the road. One of the branches hit her in the face, and she flew off the balcony. I turned and ran. I've been running ever since."

I completely forgot about my earlier accusation. I walked forward and gave her a hug.

"Parker, I'm impressed you were able to come back here after that. That must have taken a lot of courage."

She looked me in the eye. "I thought, if anywhere would have a clue as to who the traitor is, or where to find them, it would be here. I want to catch her, Evelyn."

"We will," I promised, "I don't care how long it takes, but we *will* find her."

She nodded, "And I want to find my dad. Casper said he's still alive."

"We'll find him, too." Luna said, and she also gave Parker a hug.

Behind us, Daniel cleared his throat. "I don't want to interrupt, but I think we should start exploring the apartment. The Cursers will track us down eventually."

Parker nodded, "Yeah, we should start." She walked forward and threw open the door. "Welcome to my apartment."

We walked in and looked around. One half of the room was the living room. It had a TV, a couch, and one of those big armchairs. The other half was the kitchen, but, for once, I wasn't longing to check it out. In the middle of the room was a long dining table. Behind it was a hallway leading to other rooms. I could see a big window at the end of it. That was probably the fire escape Parker had been talking about.

It would have been very inviting, except for the fact that (just like the street) it was dirty and filled with cobwebs.

The strangest thing for me wasn't the fact that it was empty. It was the fact that, if people had been there two weeks ago, why was it like this? A place didn't get ruined *that* quickly after it's abandoned.

Some strange magic was at work there, and I didn't like it.

We started digging through stuff. I started in the living room: digging through the couch cushions, looking under the chairs, and moving the television so I could see behind it.

I had just dug a quarter out of the couch when I heard a high-pitched scream.

I looked up as Mason ran screaming out of the hallway.

"What?" Parker asked. There was an edge of excitement in her voice. "Did you find something?"

"There's a . . . a . . . " Mason took a deep breath. "Dead mouse!"

She looked enraged. "Seriously?!"

Luna chose that time to come over to our side of the room from the kitchen. "This isn't going to make you feel better, but I would not recommend eating anything out of your fridge." Parker groaned and sat down on the couch. A cloud of dust flew up into the air. She didn't flinch.

She sighed. "I thought if we could find a clue anywhere, it would be here. But there's nothing but dirt and dust."

Luna shook her head. "No, there's something here. One of the lesser-known powers of a Speaker is the ability to tell if there's magic at work in an area." She twirled a finger in the air. "There's a lot of magic right here, and it's really powerful."

"Cursers," Daniel said. "They're up to something, aren't they?"

Just then, I heard a knock on the door. We all froze.

"What was that?" I whispered.

"I think," Mason said, "that was our doom knocking on the door."

Parker shook her head. "*Try* to be positive."

There was another knock.

I walked slowly towards the door and put my hand on the doorknob.

"Evelyn," Luna whispered urgently, "what are you doing? You're going to get us killed!"

I slowly turned the handle and pulled the door open.

Boom! In a flash of light and heat, I was thrown across the room and hit, what I assumed, was one of the dining chairs.

I scrambled to my feet and looked at the door of the apartment. Standing there was a tall man who was staring in amazement at something to my right.

"Dad?" I looked over and saw that Parker's face was in shock.

The guy at the door slowly nodded. "Parker? What are you doing here?" He looked around at the rest of us. "Who are these people?"

Instead of responding, she ran forward and gave him a hug. When it was over, he stepped back and examined his daughter. It was clear to see that he was still shocked that she was there.

"It's a long story that I can tell you later." Parker said, tears streaming down her face. "What are you doing here?"

"I've been trying to figure out what happened to the neighbors. The Cursers knocked me out, and, as soon as I woke up, I ran around the city trying to see if I could find you. When I got back, everyone was gone. It's been like this ever since."

Luna stepped forward. "Mr. Thomas, I'm assuming you're Mr. Thomas, the Cursers have been more active lately. They're planning something. I don't know what it is, but, knowing them, it can't be good."

He nodded. "I've noticed that. And, Parker, it seems like you have some explaining to do."

We spent the next few minutes listening to Parker tell her dad about what had happened. When she was done, he nodded slowly. "Your mother will be relieved when I tell her you're okay. The two of us and your two younger siblings have been staying in a hotel nearby. I've been coming over here daily to see if anything changed. Before today, it was nothing. Now, however, you've come back." He grinned, "It's the best thing I could've hoped for."

"One thing," Parker said.

"What?"

"You told me that my older siblings went to a boarding school in Michigan. You would never tell me what it was called or let me visit. I'm assuming they're at Enchantia?"

He nodded. "They are. And I've wanted to tell you and all your siblings for years, but they had that rule."

I stepped forward. "Why did they make that rule? What happened?"

He sighed. "People talk about the Cursers like they've been around forever: That's not true. They were only founded about sixty years ago when an Enchanter started learning dark magic. No one knows why or how, but they did. Over time, they started practicing this dark magic and teaching it to the younger students at Enchantia. When the eight Leaders found out, they sent the person away."

"But that didn't stop them," I guessed.

"Not at all. In fact, the Enchanter got so mad that they started looking for people to help them get revenge on the school. They would find a group of kids practicing magic in their neighborhood and convince them to join them. If they refused, most were taken as prisoners. A few were able to escape, but it didn't happen often. Over time, they started calling themselves the Cursers because a curse is the name for a dark spell. The Leaders of Enchantia soon realized that when a kid was caught by the Cursers, it was because they were caught using magic. So they decided that, until further notice, parents couldn't tell their kids until their thirteenth birthday. After that, they would be taken to Enchantia for five years. Anyone who found out early would go too. It's been like that ever since."

"We could find a different solution," I said. "There's always more than one way."

"I agree with Evelyn," Luna said. "We have to change this."

"We're trying," Mr. Thomas said, "but no one has come up with anything else."

"Then we need to keep trying until we do!" Parker said, practically yelling. "You can't lose hope."

"Yeah!" Mason gestured towards Parker's dad. "You probably thought that you would never see Parker again, but she's standing right here next to you."

I looked at Austin, who was silently nodding his head, and at Daniel, who was thinking so hard I could almost see the gears in his head turning.

Luna laughed. "Come up with any ideas, Dan?" she teased him.

He shook his head. "Absolutely nothing."

Mr. Thomas locked eyes with Parker through her glasses. "Where are you going to go?"

"We need to find out who let the Cursers into Enchantia," she said. "And somehow make them confess."

"Well, I don't know anything," he said, "but I know someone who might have some ideas: the one person who keeps an eye on everything and everyone."

"Who?" Mason asked.

"You need to speak to Raven Emerald, Chosen One of Enchantia."

For a moment, there was silence, but then Mason held up both hands.

"Hold on," he said. "You mean you want us to talk to *the*

Raven Emerald, Chosen One of Enchantia?"

"The person who runs the school of magic, who thinks we are the traitors who let the Cursers in?" Parker said.

Daniel shook his head. "How could we do that?"

However, I was already thinking. "What if," I said slowly, "we told her that we would like to have a private talk to explain that it's not us. Maybe if we could convince her then she would help."

"What if we sent her a letter?" Austin suggested. "Explaining that we are innocent and would like to meet with her . . . *somewhere.*"

"That is actually not a bad idea," Luna said. "Does anyone have a pencil?"

Half an hour later, with everyone gathered in the living room, I read off what I had written down.

Dear Raven Emerald,

Last Friday, the Cursers attacked the island of Enchantia. That was also the same day I arrived with my friend Parker Thomas. After the attack, we were no longer on the island. That is because a group of the Cursers was chasing us, and we had no choice but to escape. I know it looks bad. However, we would like a chance to explain our side of the story. So, we would appreciate it if you met us by the docks on the Detroit River at noon this Thursday.

Since today is Tuesday, it gives you a day to read over this letter. Please give us another chance. We would be really thankful for it.

Sincerely,

Evelyn Autumn, Parker Thomas,

Luna Everett, Daniel Crawford, Austin Hunt, and Mason Remington

"Why is my name last?" Mason demanded.

"Because *someone* had to go last," Parker said.

"Other than the order of the names," I interrupted, "does anyone have anything to comment on?"

They all shook their heads. "I think that it's pretty good," Luna said.

"Just one thing," Mason said, "why is my name—"

"Enough with the name thing!" Parker glared at him, and his mouth snapped shut.

"Moving on," I said, "how do we get it to her?"

"Leave that to me," Daniel said, reaching over and taking the letter out of my hand. He folded it up and stuck it into an envelope. (Quick reminder: the Thomas's stuff had not been removed from Parker's apartment. So, yes, they had envelopes.) He wrote on it *Raven Emerald* in neat handwriting.

"In the magic world," Daniel explained, "you don't need to

write the address. We also don't need post offices. All you have to do is write the person's name on the envelope and do this."

He waved it through the air, and the letter disappeared. Just a simple, quick swipe and it was gone.

I loved magic.

"Cool," Parker said.

"So, now," I said, "we have to go all the way back to Detroit."

"Once this is all over," Luna said, "Legend, Aqua, and Storm are getting a nice long rest in the stables."

"I think they deserve it," Daniel said.

"Definitely," I agreed, "but for right now, we need to be leaving."

"You're leaving already?" Mr. Thomas frowned at Parker.

"I'm sorry, Dad," she said, "but I have to."

He slowly nodded and sighed. "Fine, but you better be careful, okay? I don't want to lose you."

"I don't want to lose you either, Dad." Parker said and gave him a hug. "I'll be back, I promise."

We stepped onto the sidewalk to find that it had started raining. I looked around at all the broken-down buildings and couldn't help but picture horror movie posters. I had never been able to watch those films because I couldn't even get through the trailer without wanting to hide under my bed covers.

That's why I was so happy once we got out of there. The rest of the city of Chicago was not nearly as scary. In fact, even in the rain, it was still beautiful.

After finding out that her dad was okay, Parker had a lot of energy. Apparently, Storm and Mason also shared her energy, because, soon, the rest of us found ourselves racing them through the skies of Chicago.

As the city faded into the distance behind us, Mason turned around and yelled, "Good-bye, my city!"

"*Your* city?" Parker questioned. "I'm the one that *lives* here."

"Yeah, but it's the *Windy City*."

She rolled her eyes. "That's not what they mean when they say 'Windy City'."

"Sure it is."

"No, it's not."

"Yes, it is."

"No, it isn't."

After a little while, they stopped arguing, and we settled down to smooth flying.

We got bored and talked about whatever came to mind: What we liked to do in our free time, what our favorite things were, how boring school was. At one point, we passed over an ice cream shop, and the conversation turned to desserts.

Detroit appeared out of nowhere. One second it was open

sky, the next second: There it was.

We landed in a small street near the docks and set up camp in a small, empty alley. Instead of immediately going to bed, we sat and talked for a while. We meant to have someone stay up to keep watch, but, soon, we were all snoring away.

That was a huge mistake.

CHAPTER 11

FRIENDS ARE AWESOME

I knew the second I woke up that something was wrong.

My hands were tucked behind me at an awkward angle. I tried to pull them apart, but something was fighting against me.

It was a small rope. My hands were tied behind my back.

I opened my eyes and clumsily sat up as best as I could with my hands tied behind my back.

I looked into the faces of six Cursers.

"Well," Casper said, sounding annoyed. "It looks like *someone* has woken up early.

As I looked around at the dark-robed Cursers around me, I realized that they weren't all adults. The youngest one was a girl who looked just a little bit younger than I was. She stood up straight and proud like she was *happy* to be a Curser.

I glared at them. "How did you know we were here?"

"We have spies," Casper replied. "Isn't that what you're looking for? You're trying to figure out who our spy is."

"Yeah," I said, "Are you just now figuring that out? Because, if so, you're a little bit slow."

He raised his eyebrows at me. "A little slow?"

"I was trying to be nice."

From the look on his face, I'm pretty sure he wanted to kill me. "Well, girly, you can quit the tone because you're in our hands now. We won't tolerate that kind of talk."

"I'm not in anyone's hands but my own," I retaliated. "And neither are my friends."

I looked at them asleep next to me and screamed at the top of my lungs. There were a lot of things I was bad at, but being loud was something I did great.

Five sets of eyes jolted open, and, for a moment, there was just confused screaming.

"What's happening?" Parker yelled. She looked at all of the Cursers gathered around us, and her eyes grew to twice their normal size.

"Let us go, or else!" Mason's voice squeaked on the last word.

The Cursers laughed at him, but, luckily, for me, my new friends were tougher than they looked.

Slowly, each using a slightly different method, they all managed to sit up. Unfortunately for Parker, when she tried to sit up, her glasses fell off her face.

"Seriously?" she groaned.

"Who do you think you are?" Mason asked, "sneaking up on

us while we're asleep. You could at least have given us a fair chance."

"I've already told you, my name's Casper Richmond, a Curser," he said, "and there is no such thing as a fair chance. Why? Because we have powers too."

He snapped his fingers, and the world dissolved around me.

Suddenly, I was standing in a familiar school playground, and little kids, about seven or eight years old, were running around me. None of them noticed I was there.

My attention was drawn to a little girl a few feet away from me. She had curly brown hair and bright blue eyes.

It was me five years ago.

A few feet away from her (Do I say her or me?) was a group of children pointing at another kid a little distance away.

"Look at that guy," one of them said. "Special needs kids are so ugly."

"Hey!" Little me marched up to them and put her hands on her hips. "There's nothing wrong with special ed people."

He raised his eyebrows at her. "Yeah, I bet you're one too. I mean, aren't you in special speech classes?"

The group of kids ran away laughing. She watched them walk away and looked around her at the other kids on the small playground. Everyone else was playing and having fun, but her? She had no one, absolutely no one.

I noticed a single tear falling down young Evelyn's face. She quickly wiped it away. "Don't cry," she chided herself. "Crying is for weak people."

It didn't show it, but I knew what happened next. I would spend the next few years of my life longing for a friend, knowing that I was different from the rest. I would wander around, lonely, wondering if it would always be like this. I would pour through books, wanting to escape into a world where people understood my pain. It didn't seem like anyone in my world did.

The scene faded, and I was back in my house, about a year later, with my parents gathered next to me on the couch. I braced myself, preparing to relive the pain of my past.

That's when I heard the crying. The weird part was, it wasn't me or my parents, but it sounded familiar.

I focused on the sound of that crying, and, slowly, my world of pain melted around me.

I was standing back in Detroit with the Cursers in front of me. On either side of me, all my friends' eyes were closed, and tears were streaming down their faces.

Somehow, by focusing on my friends' needs, I had pulled myself out of the Curser's spell.

I locked eyes with Casper.

"How . . . how did you–" he stuttered.

"Do that?" I smiled at him. "Honestly, no idea."

I screamed, and a giant wave of water erupted out of the ground.

The Cursers screamed as the wave swept them off their feet and carried them out of the alley.

Since Casper was no longer focusing on his curse, it died. My friend's eyes snapped open.

Parker stared forward with her eyes wide open. "What was that?" she whispered.

"A stupid curse," I replied, my voice shaking. "We need to go, now."

Austin's eyes were glazed over, but he set his hands on fire, and it burned through the rope. He rummaged through Parker's bag and pulled out her pocket knife. Then, he set the rest of us free. We slowly packed up our stuff in a giant daze. None of us talked unless we absolutely needed to.

Inside my head, I wondered what they had seen.

Instead of taking the horses, which would have attracted the Cursers' attention, we just decided to walk through Detroit towards the port.

None of us had fully recovered yet. Luna and Mason still had tears streaming down their faces, Daniel kept wincing, Austin's eyes were staring off into space, and the few words Parker said were in whispers.

Watching them, I realized something. My whole life, I had gone through hard things. Feelings and emotions so complicated that they were impossible to explain in words.

Because of that, I never opened up to people. I just figured they wouldn't listen, that they wouldn't understand.

But these people had gone through difficult things too.

Maybe I could talk to them?

"What did you guys see?" I asked.

"I saw my parents dropping me off at daycare on the morning they died," Mason said. "I also got a lot of bad memories from all the different foster homes I went to."

"Obviously the memory of the Cursers coming to my apartment," Parker said, "and a few rough times I'd had in my childhood."

The time was now or never.

"I'm autistic," I blurted out.

Everyone looked over at me. Austin mouthed, *You're telling them?*

"You have autism?" Parker asked.

I looked down at my feet. "Yeah, but I don't like to talk about it. Most people either ignore kids with autism or think that they are stupid and ugly. Trust me, I see it daily."

"You aren't stupid or ugly," Luna said. "Those guys are liars."

"People like to judge people who are different from them,"

Parker said. "I hate that. It's not right."

"Yeah," Daniel agreed. "Back at my school, people would get teased for everything that made them different. Their grades, height, weight, disabilities, gender, speech, or basically anything that made one person stand out from the rest."

"Sometimes people made fun of me because I moved schools a lot," Mason said. "They teased me because I didn't have a mom or dad."

We all stared at him.

"Um," I said, "they teased you for being an orphan?"

"How low are these people?" Parker spoke so loud she was almost screaming. "Teasing someone about things they struggle with! Why would someone do that?" Judging from the look on her face, I was pretty sure she was thinking of a million different ways to kill someone.

I'd been right. There was a group of people who would stand up for me: people who had also been through some rough things themselves. They understood what it was like to feel alone and rejected.

I wanted to burst out crying and give them all hugs. Where had they been all my life?

After years of hoping to make a friend, I'd made five, all of whom were amazing people.

I already loved them.

CHAPTER 12

A MEETING WITH THE CHOSEN ONE

We set up camp next to the port. Surprisingly, nothing happened that night except we slept and took turns keeping watch.

When I woke up the next morning, the only people waiting for me were Parker and Mason, who were trying to decide what to summon on the magic plates for breakfast.

"We should have pancakes," Parker was saying. "We've had eggs almost every morning."

"I could eat eggs for breakfast, lunch, and dinner every day of the week," Mason said. "They're really good! Especially with bacon. We should have bacon too!"

"I like eggs too. Just not every day of the week."

"Um . . ." I started. "Good morning."

They both glanced over.

"Good morning," Mason replied.

"It *is* a good morning," Parker said. "Especially for trying new things like pancakes."

Mason glared at her.

In just a few minutes, we were all awake.

We ended up eating chocolate chip pancakes (Mason changed his mind as soon as I said the pancakes should have chocolate chips in them) and discussing who should do the talking when we met with Raven Emerald.

If you can call it discussing: When I asked who should explain, everyone else just yelled: "Not it!"

I was perfectly fine with doing it. I am one of those weird people who volunteer for the things no one else wants to do. Like whenever my old teachers would have students present something in front of the class, my hand always shot up into the air.

(Unless it's taking out the garbage. I won't volunteer for that.)

Pretty soon, we were standing on the docks, waiting to meet with the Chosen One of Enchantia. Once I was there, I was pretty nervous. It's not everyday you have to explain to the leader of Enchantia that you're innocent of letting Cursers into their magical school. It's even harder after you horse-napped some pegasi, stole a couple of things from the kitchen, and had been running for a few days.

Yeah, it was going to be lots of fun.

Something else fun, it was snowing again. If you have ever stood next to water while it's snowing, you know how cold that is. I felt like a human popsicle.

Daniel spotted it first. "A boat!"

Sure enough, there was a boat. Just a small fishing boat, and, as it got closer, I could see Mr. Hudson behind the wheel with the Chosen One herself sitting in a seat near him.

I was so nervous that I felt like running and hiding in a hole.

"That's Raven Emerald!" Mason yelped.

"Well, obviously!" Parker said. "Who were you expecting?"

The boat pulled up to the dock, and Raven stepped out. She was wearing a long, golden robe on top of jeans and a sweatshirt.

She stepped out of the boat onto the dock, her expression uptight and regal. I looked at my friends on either side of me. All of them looked as nervous and tense as I felt, except for Luna. Her eyes were narrowed angrily, and her jaw was set in a firm line.

"Hello, Raven," Luna said slowly, making the vowels longer than they needed to be.

"Well, hello, Luna." Raven looked at her, sizing her up. "I don't suppose this is because you are still mad at me about what happened a few months ago?"

"I promise you it's not," Luna replied, "but you still should have listened to me. If you had, they might still be here right now."

I was very confused.

"I saved you that day!" Raven glared at Luna, and, suddenly, the thought of hiding in a hole seemed like even more of a good idea.

"Well you didn't save them!" Luna yelled.

Parker looked at me with her mouth hanging wide open. She mouthed, *What the heck*?

I didn't have an answer for her, but, if the fighting continued, we were going to be out of luck.

"Um, hey, guys?" I stuttered, "Luna? Raven Emerald?"

They both turned and looked at me.

"Can we go find a place to sit down?" I asked. "We have some things to tell you."

"Fine," Luna said and looked at Raven. "You and I can discuss this some other time."

She nodded. "There are other things we need to talk about right now."

I had to resist the urge to yell: "What the heck happened to you two?"

Unfortunately for my impatient brain, I had the feeling I was going to have to wait for a little bit.

We found a nearby Mexican restaurant and decided to eat there with Raven. (Mr. Hudson was staying back to watch the boat.)

I'm pretty sure we looked like we were up to no good. I mean, seven minors walking into a restaurant with no adults sounds pretty suspicious to me. They couldn't refuse to seat us, though, so we were able to get a table.

We got a round table in the front corner next to a window and ordered our food.

I told Raven the entire story: the flood, meeting Parker, going to Enchantia, running away, and finally coming up with the idea to meet with her. The only thing I left out was what had happened the day before.

After I finished, she sat silently for a minute, considering whether or not she thought the story was real or fake.

In the end, she nodded at me with admiration. "It would take a lot to come up with that much detail so quickly. I've decided to take your word for it." She leaned forward. "Now, you wanted my opinion on who you think this spy is, right?"

All six of us nodded our heads and murmured agreement.

"Well," she started, "my first guess is actually one of the Early Magics." She glanced at Austin. "I think you might know who she is. Her name is Carly Hunt."

Austin looked shocked. "N-no," he stammered, "No, she . . .she would never do that. She's my little sister. I know she's not a spy."

Raven raised her eyebrows at him. "Do you want to hear my

reasoning?"

"Yes, please explain to me how you think you know my baby sister better than I do."

"First off, Carly didn't show up to dinner on the night the Cursers attacked. She claimed that she was sick in bed. However, she had just spent the past few hours swimming at the pool and playing in the snow. So how did she suddenly become sick?"

"I . . .I don't know, maybe she . . . ate something bad?" he said quietly.

"Right before dinner?"

"Okay, maybe not."

"Secondly, when she arrived at Enchantia, a door didn't show up for her."

"Wait, wait, wait," Luna interrupted. "A door didn't show up for her?"

Raven shook her head. "It never did."

"Let me guess," I said. "This is another result of the Cursers?"

"Actually," Raven said, "believe it or not, she's the only one who doesn't have a door. Carly's been staying in one of the guest rooms."

"Listen, Austin," Daniel looked at him nervously. "I hate to admit it, but Raven's got a point."

Austin stared at his shoes under the table.

"Is there anything else we need to know?" I asked.

Raven shook her head. "No, as far as I know, that's everything."

"Um . . . Raven Emerald?" Austin asked quietly.

She turned to him. "Yes, Austin?"

"Do you have any other guesses on who the spy may be?" he asked hopefully.

"I have some others," she said, "but none of the other guesses seem as likely as my first. I've been keeping an eye on a sixteen year old Forestus who keeps sneaking out at night. But she helped out when the Cursers attacked. There's also a fourteen year old Windy who can be quite a handful."

She stopped and shook her head. "I'm sorry, Austin, but your sister seems to be the most likely one in this scenario. All the other Enchanters that I have suspected don't have the same amount of evidence."

Austin continued to examine his shoes. I felt really sorry for him. His little sister, who he had grown up with, might be working against him and the rest of his family.

"Now, I actually have a question for you," Raven said. "Being the Chosen One of Enchantia, I am the head boss. You guys have told me your story, and I believe you. If you want, you guys could come back to Enchantia right now, and the Leaders and I could take over trying to figure out who it is."

I thought about the prophecy that Luna had spoken a few

days before. It had been about us, that much was clear. We needed to do this, not someone else.

Before I could say anything, Luna said it for me. "No," she said, "We appreciate it, but this is our job."

A faint smile tugged at the corner of Raven's mouth. "Well, then, once you guys figure it out, come back to Enchantia. Maybe you guys are the key to the problem that we've been having. There's clearly something important behind that door, I know it."

I thought about saying something about that. That I was just one twelve year old girl: How could I be their solution?

Then, I thought about what had happened the past few days. Maybe this was the big chance I had always secretly been waiting for? A chance to prove that I wasn't just a small nobody from nowhere.

"On other topics," Raven leaned forward across the table, and we did the same. "I know how you can get some more information."

"You do?" I asked.

She nodded, "Every Thursday, the most important Cursers have a meeting at their base after dark. I saw a vision about it not too long ago. If you could listen in, you might get the information you've been looking for."

Luna's vision, I thought.

"Do you know where the base is?" Daniel asked, but I

thought I could hear an edge to his voice.

She slowly nodded. "I've never been able to get into it, but I know the location."

I felt like jumping up and down and cheering. She knew where it was!

"Really?" Parker asked excitedly.

Raven smiled for real and nodded. "They put the entrance to their hideout on the highest point in Tennessee. It's called Clingman's Dome."

"How can we trust that you're telling the truth about all this?" Luna interrupted. "How do we know that you're not lying?"

Raven didn't look surprised by the question. "I'll use this."

Out of her pocket she pulled a small, glowing green crystal.

"Do you know what this is?" she asked.

"It's a lie detector," Daniel said, "It will turn red once you lie."

"Exactly," Raven looked at Luna. "Do you believe me now?"

"I will," she said, "as soon as you promise that you have never been to the Curser's hideout."

"I have never been to the Curser's hideout."

The rock stayed green.

"See? Not lying."

Luna didn't look convinced, but she nodded anyway. "Yeah, I know you can't cheat your way out of that."

"Good," Raven stood up and handed Luna the lie detector. "I

know you guys will do well. Good luck, Enchanters."

We all said goodbye, and Raven walked out the door, leaving us alone in the restaurant.

Parker turned towards Luna. "What was that all about?"

Luna sighed, "It's a long story."

"I like long stories," Mason said, "and we've got time." He tapped his wrist. "I'm in no rush to run through the Cursers' home. It doesn't sound like it's going to be much fun anyway."

"I don't want to talk about it. It's just a little something between Raven and I."

"Please tell us!" Mason begged.

Just as Luna opened her mouth to argue, the door of the restaurant burst open, and Casper the Curser and his friends came in.

All six of us crouched down in our seats, trying to stay hidden from sight.

"On second thought," Mason whispered, "we can talk later."

CHAPTER 13

AN ENTRANCE IN THE MOUNTAINS

Luckily, we got a table in the front corner and not the back. Trust me, if we had, it would have had a totally different outcome. I felt like cheering when the waitress took the Cursers to a table in the back.

We left our money on the table and snuck out, leaving a pretty good-sized tip. After walking for a few minutes, we located Legend, Aqua, and Storm hiding in an alley.

I'll admit, I was a little anxious to get back to the wilderness. I grew up in the countryside. All this city stuff wasn't for me.

You would've thought that one of us would have bothered Luna about her past with Raven during that flight, right?

Nope. I'm pretty sure we all forgot about it as soon as we took off into the air. We were headed straight for the Cursers' hideout. If any of us had opened our mouths, I'm pretty sure all that would've come out was doubt about what we were going to do.

As we flew, the sun started creeping closer to the horizon. Below us, the ground changed from snowy fields to big hills to giant mountains.

The Appalachian Mountains truly were beautiful. Miles upon miles of blue mountain peaks dominated the landscape. The snow below us seemed to shine with the late evening light. Frozen rivers weaved through the valleys.

The only bad thing was the cold. The wind went straight through my coat, chilling me to the bone. I thought about the common area back at the Enchantia Castle, filled with comfy couches and warm fireplaces. Man, I wished I was there right then.

But we had other things to do. We were headed straight for the Cursers. The plan was to find the entrance, get in, get the information we needed, and escape without being caught. Then, go back to Enchantia and convince them of what we had seen.

A flawless plan, right?

(Hey, it didn't involve alarm clocks, so there was a chance that I wouldn't mess it up.)

Luna, of course, riding on Legend, turned around and said, "This is it, guys, the next mountain."

By this point, what with their ability to sense magic and have visions, I was pretty sure it was impossible to hide anything from Speakers.

We flew over the top of one of the mountains, and, suddenly, Legend dove. Storm and Aqua followed on their own.

I looked down at the mountain we were approaching. I could make out a trail heading towards the summit. Because of how cold it was, I wasn't surprised to see that no one was on it.

We touched down in the middle of the trail, and, as everyone else slid effortlessly off, I toppled into the snow. I'm a very graceful rider.

As I brushed the snow off my coat, I looked around. There wasn't any clear indicator that there was magic anywhere nearby. Like every other mountain we'd passed, there were piles of snow, frost on the trees, and rocks everywhere.

Daniel looked at Luna. "You sense magic?"

She nodded, "Lots of it. Curser magic, not Enchanter magic. The Cursers may have once been Enchanters, but the magic is *completely* different."

"So," Mason said, "where is this entrance? I'm ready to get inside."

Parker shifted nervously. "I don't know. Don't you remember Luna's vision? I personally would like to avoid a fight. I hate fights."

"You were fine with fighting when the Cursers attacked Enchantia," I pointed out.

"That was different. They were on our land, and we probably would have had to fight them anyway. I wasn't going to sit up in my room waiting for an ambush!"

"Well, we're this close. We can't turn back now." I turned to Luna. "How do we get in?"

Instead of answering right away, she turned and walked towards the cliff face behind us.

She rubbed her hand across the bare rock. "It's right here, I can feel it."

"Maybe we need, like, a code or something?" Daniel wondered aloud.

That gave me an idea. "Stand back," I demanded. Luna stepped away from the wall, and I walked forward.

I knocked a pattern on the wall:

Knock. Pause. *Knock knock.* Pause. *Knock.*

It was the code that the Curser had knocked on the library door when we had been cornered. I know what you're thinking, *How did you remember that*? Well, dear reader, my brain likes to remember random facts. Numbers, patterns, book/movie quotes: Those things stick inside my head.

Sometimes, like that day, that pays off.

A ten foot tall crack sliced up the cliff face. The ground shook under our feet, and, slowly, the two chunks of rock slid apart to reveal: a dark tunnel.

"Seriously?" Parker muttered under her breath.

"Wait a minute," Austin said. He slid his red robe off his shoulders and stuffed it into the bag on his back.

"Good idea," Daniel said, and did the same for his robe.

I made a mental note to ask later why Luna and Mason didn't have a robe.

"Come on, Enchanters!" Mason announced, "Fun awaits!"

He marched straight into the tunnel, and, reluctantly, the rest of us followed.

It was a good thing he was with us. Without him, we probably would have gotten only a few feet in before retreating, but he didn't stop or slow down. He marched through with confidence. Where he got that from, I didn't know.

We walked for only about a minute before we emerged into the main hideout area and froze in our tracks.

It was definitely not what I'd been expecting.

I still preferred Enchantia, but it was an amazing sight. The ceiling, hundreds of feet up, was decorated with a night sky even more beautiful than the real one. The cavern was filled with winding roads that connected small buildings to form a nighttime village. At the end of the main road we were standing on was a grand castle, only slightly smaller than the Enchantia one.

It really made me wonder. These were the bad guys? This was the secret hideout we'd been looking for? How could something so beautiful belong to a group who had done such bad things?

Priorities, Evelyn, I chided myself. *Don't focus on the pretty architecture. That's not what is important right now.*

I turned towards my friends, who were also gaping at the impressive cavern.

"Shouldn't we . . . ?" I waved my hands around, trying to get out what my mouth couldn't seem to say. Shouldn't we get going on doing the dangerous stuff? Shouldn't we not stand around staring at an enemy's base, even though it was grand and majestic?

"Get going?" Parker suggested.

"Yeah."

We walked down the main road, and everywhere I looked I saw Cursers in dark robes. For some reason, they were all staring at us.

Then I looked down and realized why they were staring. I was still wearing my bright coat (yellow, it's an amazing color) and black leggings with the usual dirty sneakers. It was what I normally wore, because I didn't really care that much about my appearance.

But, at that moment, I realized our outfits might be the thing that would give us away. They were all wearing dark robes, and I just walked in there with my bright yellow.

Stupid, Evelyn, I chided myself again.

I glanced around at the buildings on the main street. Many of them were shops. There was a potion shop, a magical garden shop, a library (Which, even in that dangerous moment, I was tempted to check out.), and . . . *Bingo!* A robes shop.

I turned towards my friends, who were all glancing nervously at the Cursers.

"Guys!" I whispered urgently, "On the right!"

We all changed direction and walked to the front of the store.

After just a few minutes, we were ready. I walked out of the shop with the hood pulled over my head.

We blended in with the crowd. Huddled close together, we cautiously made our way down the street, careful not to look anyone in the eyes.

I'll admit, I had a hard time focusing. I kept glancing at shop windows as we walked past.

Sure, what we were doing may have been dangerous, and it may have ended very badly, but all I could think was: *This is so cool*! As someone who grew up on fantasy books, a beautiful secret cavern filled with people who could do magic was like a dream come true.

Poor, innocent, young Evelyn, if only I had known that doing magic came with a price.

We reached the doors of the castle, and I grabbed the handle. Cautiously, I opened the door.

The feel of the Cursers' castle was totally different from the Enchanters'. The floor beneath our feet was dark oak. The walls of the entrance hall were dark gray. Instead of the cozy chairs and fireplaces, there were suits of polished armor lined up on either side of us. A red carpet spread down the middle towards a grand double staircase at the end.

There were a few similarities, though. Above our heads gleamed a beautiful chandelier, but gold, as opposed to the crystal one in the Enchantia library. In between the sets of stairs was a roaring fireplace.

The weirdest thing about it though? It didn't feel scary or dangerous or like a place that could get you in a lot of trouble. If anything, it felt *welcoming*. It was like walking into a fairy-tale castle. I wouldn't have been surprised to hear that royalty lived here.

We walked down the carpet towards the stairs, because where else were we supposed to go?

We reached the set of stairs on the right, and Luna said, "Guys, stop for a minute."

The rest of us turned to her. She looked slightly nervous, but when she spoke I couldn't detect fear in her voice.

"I had another dream last night. In the dream, it showed me where we needed to go. So even when it may seem like we're lost, you have to trust me, okay?"

"Okay," I said. "You ready to do some eavesdropping?"

"Not really," Parker said, "but I don't think we have much of a choice."

"Then let's go," I said.

We followed Luna up the stairs, and she took an immediate right. As we walked, I tried to keep track of where we were going: right, left, left, right, up a flight of stairs, another left. Eventually, I lost track of where we were.

I saw what Luna meant when she said, "*When it may seem like we're lost.*" I certainly felt lost.

Eventually, we came to a long hallway, and Luna stopped and turned around.

"This is it?" I guessed.

She nodded. "We have to be quiet."

"But we're going to get caught anyway," Daniel pointed out, "That's what you saw in your vision."

"We don't know that we don't get away," Luna retaliated. "I never saw evidence of that."

"I don't like your powers of sight," Mason said, "They seem kind of . . . I don't know . . . unreliable?"

"There are some things that should never be revealed, even to Speakers. Because, if something unpleasant happens, we may try to stop it from happening and make the situation worse."

"You're not helping my nerves."

"I know, but I'm not lying."

"Okay," I interrupted before we ran out of time. "Shouldn't we get going?"

"We should," Luna agreed.

We silently crept down the hallway. It surprised me that a group of middle schoolers could *be* so quiet. It wasn't something that we're really known for.

Soon, I heard talking coming from behind one of the doors. Out of the corner of my eye, I saw Daniel reach over and grab Luna's hand.

Aww, I thought, but I didn't say anything.

We reached the door the talking was coming from and put our ears up against it.

"–keep getting away," a voice was saying, and I recognised it. It was Casper, for the millionth time.

He was really getting on my nerves.

"We'll get them eventually," a new voice said, "Just be patient."

"Why do we even *need* them?" a third voice said. "Couldn't Carly just get it for us? She knows where it is! Why can't she bring it to us herself?"

I turned towards my friends, whose eyes were bigger than ever. We all stared at each other. So now we knew who it was. What did we do with the information?

Suddenly, I noticed a tear falling down Austin's cheek. Then it hit me:

The spy, the one that we had been looking for, *was his little sister.*

He shook his head. "Guys, it's not true!" he whispered urgently. "It can't be. Carly would never, *ever* do this."

Next to me, Mason twitched suddenly, and I looked over at him. Unfortunately, I recognised what he was about to do a little too late.

He leaned his head back and– "Ah-CHOO!"

(Be glad you have never heard Mason sneeze. It is the equivalent to a dying vacuum cleaner.)

The voices in the room stopped.

"What was that?" a voice asked.

"I'll check," Casper answered.

We all jumped away from the door, and it burst open. I did the natural thing. I thrust one hand in front of me and summoned a jet of water that propelled him backwards into the room.

The six of us sprinted down the hallway. Behind me, I heard Casper yell. "Get them!"

From somewhere inside the castle, I heard a giant bell ringing. It was definitely an alarm.

Luna led the way, speeding down hallways and showing us where we needed to go. At that moment, I was glad she had such a good memory.

Suddenly, we reached the dead end of a hallway, and on either side of us were two different hallways leading away into other parts of the castle.

Luna froze with a horrified expression on her face. "I . . . I can't remember which turn to take."

Suddenly, I heard something behind me and whipped around just in time to see Casper send a bolt of dark light spiraling towards us.

Austin and I dove to the left, while, out of the corner of my eye, I saw Parker, Mason, Daniel, and Luna take off to the right. Casper's bolt of light hit the wall right behind where we had previously been standing, and rubble and dust filled the hallway as that wall caved in.

Coughing and spluttering, I managed to sit up from where I had fallen onto the ground.

"Austin?" I called.

"Right here," I heard him croak, and a gentle hand grabbed my own.

The dust cleared, and I looked in front of me at the giant wall of broken stone.

"The . . . the others," I mumbled.

"We'll have to hope that they're okay," Austin replied, his voice shaking. "For right now, we have to go."

I looked at the tears streaming down his face and squeezed his hand. "Listen, Austin . . . " What could I possibly say?

"But . . . but Carly," he stared down at his hands. "She would *never* join the Cursers."

"Listen, Austin," I said slowly, "I hate to say it, but maybe you don't know her as well as–"

"They knew we were coming."

I froze and raised my eyebrows at him. "What?"

"They knew we were coming. Do you think they just happened to be talking about the spy while we were standing there?"

I stared at him. He had a point. Nothing in my life had ever been that easy.

"It was staged," he explained, "It had to be. The Cursers are trying to frame my sister."

It took a moment to let that sink in. "Why . . . why your sister?"

He shook his head. "No clue, but someone knew we were coming and took this as a golden opportunity."

"Who knew we were coming?"

The answer hit me in the face like a brick. Austin and I stared at each other for a minute as the details clicked into place in our brains.

"It couldn't be," I whispered.

"And yet, it makes sense."

"We've got to go," I stood up. "Come on, Austin. *'Fire and water combined pursue.'*"

We ran down the length of the hallway, turned a corner, and I froze, again.

Unlike the rest of the hallways we had been down, this one had tall windows on one side that looked out over the Curser's small village. In the distance, I could see the mouth of the giant cavern.

"I have an idea!" I announced to Austin.

"I know! You know who is working for the Cursers. So do I."

"No, not for that."

"For saving our friends?"

"Eventually it leads to saving them, but, first, we *es-cap-aye*!"

"Escape?"

"You say it your way, I'll say it my way."

"Okay then, so the plan?"

I pointed at the small buildings outside. "We jump out a window!"

He looked at me like I was crazy. In his defense, I am.

"Neither of us are Windys," he pointed out, "Unless your plan to escape leads to certain death."

"Just trust me on this."

He sighed, "Fine. I trust you, Evelyn."

We ran to the nearest window and threw it open. Austin grabbed my hand and squeezed it tight.

"We're not going to die."

"Just a little nervous to be—you know—jumping out a window."

Together, we leaped out into the open air. Shockingly, I wasn't scared. I knew what to do.

I concentrated, which was hard to do with Austin screaming his head off, and, in midair, we froze.

I looked down at my feet and gave a small smile. We were standing on top of a small geyser. I willed it to slowly sink back to the ground, carrying us with it.

Austin stared at me. "Evelyn Autumn, that was . . . very dangerous . . . and kinda cool?"

I gave a little bow. "Now part two, which you get to help me with."

He nodded and even gave a small grin back. "Okay, fine, now I *really* trust you. Lead the way."

But then the rest of the plan was quickly thrown out the window when I heard a familiar scream.

The small bit of hope we'd been feeling a second before faded, and I looked at Austin's pale face.

"Parker," I said, and we took off running.

Don't you hate it when your plans are thrown out the window? (Sorry, unintentional pun.) One second you know what you're doing, and the next second you're left questioning what to do.

That's pretty much what happened at that moment.

We ran through a few alleys back towards the main street, where a large crowd had gathered.

"I can't see!" I complained, jumping up and down.

"Here!" Austin grabbed my hand and dragged me towards a dumpster on the side of the road. He climbed on the lid and then helped me up.

I gasped at what I saw.

In front of the gates of the palace, Casper and his Curser friends had managed to capture *my* friends.

One Curser held Parker's tied hands behind her back. Her face hurt me the most. It looked like someone had drained all the energy out of her. Her eyes were glossed over, and all I wanted to do was run through the crowd to help her.

Mason also had his hands tied behind his back, but, instead of being dead silent like Parker, he was yelling insults at all the Cursers. They didn't seem affected at all by it though.

Since his hands were tied behind his back, Daniel kept unsuccessfully trying to kick the Cursers around him. Every time he tried, they would just dodge him.

Luna was struggling with all her might, demanding that she be let go. Tears were streaming down her face.

Casper, standing in front of the four of them, announced to

the crowd. "These Enchanters snuck in, trying to steal our most precious items! They keep coming after us, but we shall not let these other people of magic control us. The Enchanters are liars, thieves, and they wish to see our City of Cursers destroyed!" He turned towards the Cursers holding my friends. "Take them to the dungeons to await trial!"

"Wait!" Luna yelled, and everyone froze. "He's lying to you! We're not thieves trying to steal anything! We're just trying to protect our home!"

Casper sneered. "You lie, Speaker!"

"No, I don't."

Casper snapped his fingers, and she fainted.

"Luna!" Daniel shook himself free of his captors and tried to run over to her. Another snap of the fingers and Daniel fell to the ground like he had been tripped. Sprawled on the ground, his eyes stared off into space.

"Now," Casper glared at Mason and Parker. "Do either of you have anything to add?"

"We do!" I yelled, and Casper turned towards Austin and I.

Austin pointed at Casper. With the same air as someone talking about the weather, he said, "Your hair's on fire."

Casper screamed as his hair ignited at Austin's simple words.

Luna and Daniel snapped awake and sprung to their feet. Parker's eyes unglossed (Is that a word?), and she managed to throw off her captor.

I raised my hands, and the castle doors burst open. Hundreds of gallons of water flowed out down the main street. It was the biggest flood I had ever done. The crowd of Cursers screamed and started climbing on top of anything they could find to escape the raging rapids.

Mason, Parker, Luna, and Daniel shot up into the air above the water (I'm mostly sure it was Mason's doing) and hovered there.

After a minute, I made the water disappear. This time, however, there was a backlash to it.

Immediately, exhaustion swept over me. I felt like I was going to fall over at any second. My head ached. My eyelids felt heavy. I thought I might throw up.

Suddenly, my friends were by my side.

"Are you okay?" Parker asked. "You look like you're going to be sick."

"I think it's just too much power at once," I said quietly. "I'll be fine."

Mason whistled, and I turned towards the entrance to the cave just in time to see three pegasi come flying towards us.

They landed next to us. Austin helped me climb onto Aqua's back.

From behind us, I heard what had recently become the most

annoying voice in the world.

Casper yelled, "Get the invaders!"

Austin shot a ball of fire towards him. He screamed again and disappeared behind the smoke.

The horses took off into the air, Austin shooting fireballs at almost everything. Houses, shops, and flowerbeds went up in flames.

We reached the mouth of the cave, and I did the most heroic thing to do during an escape.

I fainted.

CHAPTER 14

UNFORTUNATELY, I WAS RIGHT

The first thing I saw once I woke up was Austin's bright blue eyes.

He sighed with relief. "*Finally*, you're up!"

I looked around the room we were in and saw a few faces I'd expected to see: Parker, Mason, Luna, and Daniel.

Then, I saw two faces I hadn't been expecting.

"Colten and Ellie Hunt?" I asked.

Ellie smiled. "Welcome back, my dear."

I was lying on the Hunts' couch in their living room. I recognized it from a few days before. (What *was* it now? Seven or eight?)

"What are we doing back here?" I asked.

"We didn't want to go back to Enchantia with you unconscious. So I told everyone we could stop by my house and wait until you woke up," Austin explained.

I smiled. "Thank you for that."

Although, inside my head I was thinking: *Woah! Flashback time*!

"Do you guys want to stay here for a little while?" Ellie asked. "There's enough room for all of you. Plus," she looked at the clock on the wall. "It's five in the morning, surely you don't want to go back right *now*."

"I appreciate the offer, but I don't like to wait around. We need to get going." I looked around at everyone else. "Of course, as long as everyone else is okay with that."

"I would be perfectly fine with going now," Parker said, "but are you sure? You just woke up!"

"I'm ready." Believe it or not, I wasn't lying. I felt refreshed and energized, and we had to get this over with.

I jumped off the couch. "Come on, guys, let's go."

Just a half hour later, we were soaring over Lake Erie, heading back to Enchantia.

I was nervous. I hadn't yet told everyone else who I thought it was, and Austin hadn't said a word either. It didn't make a whole lot of sense to me, but once I added up the details, it all fell into place. It was like completing a puzzle. The pieces by themselves didn't make much sense, but, once it was all together, you could see how it worked out.

Up ahead, I spotted a stretch of land on the horizon. It seemed like we were there.

It started to snow, and we landed softly on the beach.

I looked ahead at the Castle of Enchantia in front of us. The tallest tower glowed with its strange light. I noticed for the first time that, unlike the other towers, it didn't have any windows. That was strange.

We dismounted the pegasi, and I put a hand on Aqua's mane.

"Thank you," I whispered.

She nodded her head, and, along with Legend and Storm, took off flying towards the stables.

I turned towards my friends. Parker and Mason shivered in their coats, which I found weird because I wasn't at all cold.

Then, I realized that I had been sitting behind Austin on the way here. Austin could control fire. He gave off heat. No wonder I wasn't cold.

Then, I glanced at Luna and Daniel, and, in spite of how nervous I was, I had to smile.

Daniel, being a freezer, was apparently not bothered by the cold either. He was standing perfectly fine in jeans and a t-shirt. However, one of his arms was wrapped around Luna's shoulders as she stood in the snow, wearing his white robe.

Aww, I thought.

"So now we're here," Luna said, and a small part of my brain noticed her move closer to Daniel. "Who do you think it is?"

I explained to them, and watched as their eyes grew slowly bigger and bigger.

Parker shook her head. "You're forgetting one detail."

"What?" I asked.

"She said she has never been to the Cursers' hideout."

That realization sunk in, and I felt like punching myself. "Oh, that's right."

"Actually, Parker," Luna said, and, for an unknown reason, a tear fell down her cheek. "I know at the time I said you can't cheat that, but I think I may have been wrong. She's always had a way of getting out of things. It's just . . . " She sighed. "I . . . I can't believe she would do that. Especially after what happened to John and Ava."

I raised my eyebrows. "Who are John and Ava?"

"John was my brother," she said, "and Ava . . . Ava was my best friend."

I raised my hands. "I knew you had some connection to her. Later, after all of this is over, I want a full story."

She sighed again and then nodded slowly. "Okay, fine."

Parker studied me. "If you're right, it isn't going to be very easy for us to convince everyone about this."

"Yeah," Mason said. "Because everything else has been easy. Doing tricks on flying horses, running away from Enchantia, walking straight into the Curser's hideout: It was a piece of cake."

Parker gave a tiny grin. "I hate to admit it, but Mason's right. If we can do all those other things, we can do this too."

"I shall savor this moment forever!" Mason exclaimed.

Austin looked me in the eye. "What do we do now?"

"We get everyone's attention."

"I'm afraid to ask how?"

"Allow me," Mason put his fingers to his lips and let out a screeching (and I mean *screeching*) taxi cab whistle. I was pretty sure people in China had heard it.

"How can you whistle *that* loud?" I yelled at him.

"Well, you see," he started to explain. "I'm a Windy, and sound waves travel in the air, so basically–"

Never before had I been so glad to hear castle doors bang open.

Eight of the nine Leaders (Raven was missing) marched out into the snow. Behind them came tons of grumbling students. There were Oceanus, Forestus, Speakers, Healers, Flames, Windys, Freezers, and Sparks.

I recalled the way all my old classmates had stared at me after I'd slammed the band room door shut. I'd been terrified out of my mind at having that many people looking at me. Now, I longed for that kind of attention. That was nothing compared to this.

"Enchanters!" I yelled and spread my arms. "Today we have come to prove something to you! We know who let the Cursers in a few days ago!"

I scanned through the crowd, and my eyes landed on ten year old Carly Hunt. Watching her stand there, barefoot in the snow, wearing a soft pink nightgown, it seemed crazy to me that she had once been a suspect. There was no way it could ever have been her.

Then the real traitor stepped out in front of the crowd.

"Raven Emerald!" Suddenly, I was shoved aside as Luna pushed me out of the way to stand a few feet in front of us, hands on her hips. I couldn't see her face, but I could imagine the glare she was giving the "Chosen One."

"What have you *done*?"

Raven looked shocked. "What do you mean, '*What have you done*?'"

"Oh, you know what you have done." Luna reached one hand into her pocket. "You've been working with the Cursers." She took a small object out of her pocket and chucked it at Raven.

Instinctively, she reached up and caught it. "I have not been working with the Cursers."

The crowd gasped as the object changed to glow ruby red. I realized what it was. It was the lie detector Raven herself had given Luna a few days ago. She had been stabbed with her own sword.

Raven slowly lowered the rock, looking at it in a daze.

She turned and faced the bigger crowd, but I could still see the red light shining in her hand. "It's not true!" She told the crowd, and she pointed at us. "These people are the ones really working for the Cursers! The Cursers attacked the day they arrived! I have never been to the Cursers' hideout!"

The rock changed to green, and I got an idea.

"You've never been to the Cursers' hideout?" I asked her.

Raven turned to face me. "Never."

"You know, some people work from home."

She raised her eyebrows. "Yes, I know that. What does this have to do with anything?"

"You've been sending messages back and forth to them and helping them with things outside of the City of Cursers." I said, the answer forming plain and simple in my mind. "That way, you would be helping them, but if anyone ever suspected you, you could just say that you have never been to their hideout."

Raven stuck the lie detector into her pocket. "I can't believe you would suggest such a ridiculous thing! I have never worked with the Cursers."

I glared at her. "Now, say it with the rock."

She stared at me for a moment then glanced behind her at the large crowd. Slowly, Raven dug it out of her pocket. "I . . . I have never worked with the Cursers."

Once again, the entire school of Enchantia gasped as the green faded to red.

Mr. Hudson stepped forward. "Raven, how could you?"

Raven stumbled backwards away from him. "It's a lie! It's all a lie! I would never do that!"

"Then where were you when the Cursers attacked a week ago?"

"I was helping from the back lines! I was shooting fireballs and snowballs—"

"You were in the library!" Daniel glared at her. "Trying to capture us! How could you do that to Luna?"

In desperation, she locked eyes with Luna. "You know I would never do that, right?"

"Then we would've gone back." Luna sobbed, "We would've gone after them. I should've known from the moment people started rumoring about a traitor. It was you all along. You never cared for us."

Knowing she was defeated, Raven looked me in the eye and glared. "I got away with this until you showed up and ruined it."

"You chose this," I pointed out. "It's your fault. Don't blame me."

"You are a powerful one, Evelyn Autumn. Someday, you will see why I chose this way."

She snapped her fingers and was engulfed in a cloud of fire and smoke. I turned away, coughing and gasping for air. When the smoke finally disappeared, I looked back at the spot where she had previously been standing.

Raven Emerald, traitor, Leader, Chosen One, had left Enchantia.

For a few minutes, no one spoke.

After what seemed like forever, Daniel turned towards Luna and gave her a hug. "I'm sorry." I heard him whisper.

Tears streamed down her face. "I . . . I should've known. Raven never enjoyed hanging out with us. She always did her own thing. She was always distant."

Now that it was over, I was very confused. I knew most of what was going on, but the part with whatever had happened in Luna and Raven's past was still a mystery. Fortunately, not for much longer. She turned towards me. "I owe the rest of you an explanation."

Mason sighed. "And here comes depressing story time."

Mr. Hudson faced the crowd. "Everyone else, back to bed. As for you six," he turned to us. "We have some things to talk about."

We were led through the castle. Even though I had been through it before, I still had to resist the urge to gasp at the beautiful interior.

Eventually, we came to a door on the fifth floor, the Speakers level. It wasn't the bedroom hall, so I began to wonder for the first time what else was on each of the floors.

Maybe the Oceanus level has an aquarium? I thought.

An enormous castle, my brain responded, *and this is what you think of?*

Shut up, I told it.

My brain can be such a downer sometimes.

Mrs. Cordelia, the Leader of the Speakers (Luna had mentioned her during one of our discussions on the way back to Detroit from Chicago.) pulled the door open.

This time, I couldn't resist the gasp that came out.

It was a long room with a tall, curved ceiling and tall windows lining the walls. In the middle of the room was a long table with seating for twenty-one (ten chairs on each side, with a single chair at the end). On the far end of the room, behind the table, was a fireplace. A Leader wearing a red robe like Austin's flicked his hand, and it filled with a roaring fire that looked like it had been going for hours.

We all took seats at the table. It seemed like it didn't really matter where everyone sat, so I took a place in between Austin and Parker.

I noticed nobody sat in the chair at the head of the table. Then, it hit me why:

That was the Chosen One's seat. It was Raven Emerald's chair.

"First," Mr. Hudson looked me straight in the eyes. "I want to hear your story from your point of view."

I had expected this. I recounted the story as I had what seemed like a million times. This time, however, was longer than the rest. When I was done, I turned towards Luna. "Now it's time for you to tell your story."

Luna cleared her throat. "Well it all started—"

"You know," Mrs. Cordelia interrupted, "as a Speaker, there's a simpler way to show them."

She raised her eyebrows. "Are you thinking about what I think you're thinking about?"

"You can summon a vision to show them. Anything you want them to see."

Another thing I had been right about: You can't hide anything from a Speaker.

Luna shifted nervously. "But I haven't been able to do it yet."

"Just try, my dear. You said your first prophecy, correct?"

"That's correct."

"Then try it."

Luna sighed, rolled up the sleeves of her robes, took a deep breath, and held out her arms.

Slowly, purple light formed at her fingertips. It grew bigger and spiraled outwards, filling the whole room with a purple glow. She closed her eyes, and everything went black.

CHAPTER 15

VISIONS ARE NOT FUN

I was standing in the middle of what was clearly someone's bedroom. The walls were a beautiful shade of blue, the wooden floor was dark oak, and a single window on the wall looked out into the bustling streets of a city. The bed was a loft, and underneath it were three people playing a card game.

"Uno!" a girl with blonde hair yelled, mischievously smirking as she placed a card in the discard pile.

A boy with dark hair and skin grinned wickedly at her. "Nice try," he slammed down the one card left in his hand. "I win!"

The third person laughed, and I looked at her clearly for the first time, instantly recognising her.

It was Luna.

"Why is it always so competitive between you two?" she asked.

"Because it matters who is better," the girl replied and picked up the cards. "I demand a rematch!"

"You're on!" the boy replied, and the door burst open.

I scowled at the face that stuck her head in the room.

"Ava! Keep it down in here!" Raven Emerald glared at her. "I'm trying to study!"

"Okay, we will," Luna assured her, and Raven shut the door again.

"'*Keep it down!*'" Ava imitated, "'*I'm trying to study!*'" She started angrily shuffling the cards. "Study for *what*? She doesn't even go back to that stupid boarding school for another month. Besides," she looked up at Luna and the boy, who I assumed was John. "We have guests. Sometimes my older sister just needs to learn that, every once in a while, she can come and play Uno with us."

She finished dealing the cards and slammed down the first card into the deal pile. "John, you're first."

The door burst open again, and Raven ran into the room, slamming the door behind her.

"I heard that," she glared at Ava. "And I told you I'm busy."

Ava stood up, her arms crossed against her chest. "What do you even do at that school that keeps you so busy anyway? You used to be fun to be around, but ever since you became a teenager and went off to that school all you ever do is work all the time!"

"I have to, okay? One day, you'll go there too, and you'll understand–"

"Maybe I don't want to go there!"

"It doesn't matter whether you do or not! You will never have as many responsibilities as I do!"

"Then explain these 'responsibilities' that you have! Explain why you can't tell me anything about this school! *What are you hiding from me?*"

"I'm not supposed to tell you!" I was surprised to see tears fall down Raven's face.

"Why not?" Ava yelled.

"I'm trying to protect you!"

"From *what*?!"

The door to the room burst open, and yet another familiar face entered.

It was Casper wearing his same old robe.

Luna, John, and Ava screamed, backing away from the door. Raven faced him, her face instantly going pale. "What are *you* doing here?"

He grinned at her. "Ah, if it isn't Raven Emerald, the Chosen One of Enchantia."

"The what of what?" Ava yelped.

"The *Chosen One of Enchantia*," Raven rolled her eyes. "Fancy title for a lousy job."

"Is this an illusion?" Ava asked.

Casper smiled. "Not at all, Ava Emerald."

"How do you know my name?" she asked, glaring at him. I

was shocked he didn't back away in fear. I would've run if I was in a fight against that girl.

"I know a lot about you, Ava. You may just be the Cursers' key to success."

"I don't want to be the 'key to success' to someone who barges into my house pretending to be a witch."

Casper raised his eyebrows. "I am a Curser, not a witch, but there is one thing we have in common."

"What's that?" John challenged.

"We both do curses."

Ava opened her mouth, but, before she could say anything, Raven stepped in between Casper and the other three. "I am in charge while our parents are out for the night, and I will not allow this in my house."

"In charge? Again? Don't you ever get tired of being in charge?"

A little of the light seemed to die in Raven's eyes. "That's . . . that's not the point."

"It isn't, or is it?" Casper grinned at her. "Admit it, you hate being in charge."

"Raven?" Ava interrupted, "What the heck is going on?"

"Ava, stay out of this," she turned back to Casper. "And I do not!"

I heard the obvious waver on the last word.

"Let me tell you this, Raven Emerald: If you ever get tired of being in charge, come find me. All I need is a little bit of help from you, and then you can be free. Free of responsibilities. Free of stress. Free of the weight on your shoulders. I know it, this is what you want most."

"No, it's not!" Raven pointed at the wall that had the window in it, and a beam of golden light shot out of her fingertip. It hit, and the wall exploded, causing broken cement, wood, and dust to fly all over the bedroom. "I would never join you, Casper!"

She grabbed onto Luna's and Ava's hands, since John already had a hold of Ava's. "We're going to have to jump!"

"We can't jump!" John looked like he was in shock. I couldn't blame him. "We'll die!"

Casper shot a beam of dark light at them, but Raven intercepted it in the air with her own golden one.

"On the count of three! One, two, three!"

I could instantly see what went wrong.

As Raven jumped, Ava's hand slipped out of her sister's grasp, leaving John and Ava standing in the bedroom while Raven and Luna jumped to safety.

John and Ava whipped towards Casper, who chuckled at the two of them standing practically helpless.

The scene shifted, and, suddenly, I was at street level standing next to Raven and Luna. I looked up, and could see a hole in the side of the building next to us.

Luna stared at Raven. "You can *fly*?"

Raven nodded slowly, staring up at the gaping hole. "Yeah, that's not important right now."

"*Not important?*"

She was cut short when, from above, the air was filled with a loud scream. A burst of light came out of the hole in the side of the building as pieces of wood and broken cement started raining down on the street.

"John! Ava!" Luna screamed.

Raven grabbed her arm and dragged her out of the way of everything falling around them.

They collapsed on the sidewalk on the opposite end of the street, away from the apartment, Luna still screaming for John and Ava.

"Quiet!" Raven barked at her. "He's going to come after us!"

"But . . . but—"

I caught a dark shape flying out of the window, but, while it wasn't a creature I had seen before in real life, I could tell what it was.

Luna stopped struggling for a second and gaped. "Is that a *dragon*?"

"Yes."

Luna pointed angrily at Raven. "What did you do? What the

heck just happened? Is this a dream? A dragon took off with my two best friends?"

Raven shook her head, tears falling down her face. "Unfortunately, this is not a dream."

I could see the moment of realization in Luna's eyes. "Magic . . . Is it real?"

"Yeah, it's not as great as it seems."

"But . . . but," Luna looked up at the side of the building. "John, Ava," she muttered. Then, she froze and looked at Raven. "Wait, you can fly! We can go after them. We can get them back, and then you can explain all this to me!"

"No, we can't."

"What do you mean we *can't*?"

"They're in the Cursers' hands now. There's no getting them back."

Luna glared at her. "These are our *siblings*, and you're giving up?"

"You don't get it."

"You're right, I don't. I have no idea what the heck just happened. But I do know that you are letting John and Ava get kidnapped. That isn't what someone in charge would–"

"Enough with the 'being in charge' thing!" Raven yelled. "I'm tired of being put in charge of everything! For once, I would like to step back and take a break!"

"What are you talking about?" Luna asked, raising her eyebrows.

Raven sighed, "I'll fill you all in later, but for right now . . . " She grabbed Luna's hand. "We need to go. I need to get you to Enchantia."

They started walking down the street, Luna still arguing that they needed to help John and Ava.

At my feet, a wave of purple light came out of the sidewalk. It rose up into the air, filling every corner of the vision until I could see nothing else.

Everything went black, and then I was back in the room with the Leaders like nothing had ever happened.

A tear went down Luna's face. "That's . . . that's what happened.

Everything was silent. None of us knew what to say.

My story had been scary, sure. No one likes the idea of being followed by a creepy guy wearing a robe. But Luna's? Her discovery of magic was her brother and her best friend, the two people she cared about most in the world, being kidnapped by the Cursers. Months later, she had still heard nothing.

Then, Raven Emerald, Ava's older sister, joined the Cursers. I couldn't imagine being in Luna's spot right then. The amount of pain she must have been feeling: How had she been able to share that? I barely ever told anyone when something was bothering me. Telling someone about what you were going through was its own type of bravery.

The silence was broken by Daniel, who draped his arm over Luna's shoulders.

"You know," he said. "They can't be dead."

"How?" she asked. "They were kidnapped by the Cursers, and I know both of them. They wouldn't let anyone boss them around. They'd rather starve to death than be kept as prisoners."

Surprisingly, Mrs. Cordelia smiled. "You're right. They wouldn't let themselves be kept as prisoners."

Luna glared at her. "What? Do you find that amusing?"

Mrs. Cordelia propped her head up with her hand. "I had a vision myself last night."

I raised my eyebrows. "You did?"

She nodded and looked at Luna. "They escaped."

Luna's jaw dropped, but then, slowly, she started grinning. "They did?"

"Yes, they're on the run, but very much alive."

"Then we need to find them!" she exclaimed. "We need to send out search parties or do something!"

"We will find them, I promise you that." The happy expression faded from her face. "We have to, because we need them."

Parker looked concerned. "I'm scared to ask: For what?"

"As you all know, the Cursers are slowly defeating us."

I sighed. "Yeah, that *very* joyful thought keeps popping back up in my head."

She leaned forward. "Throughout all of Enchantia's history, we have cherished the number eight above all others. There are eight powers, eight Leaders. Even the amount of places at each of the tables in the dining hall is eight! It just seems like fate that in our darkest moment, when the Enchanters' powers are so faded, that eight people, each one with a different power, would show up at Enchantia like this."

One at a time, she looked each of us in the eyes. "I have had no visions or prophecies about this, but I believe you may be the answer we've been looking for."

Parker frowned. "There's a problem with that."

Mrs. Cordelia raised her eyebrows. "What?"

"Casper the Curser said pretty much the same thing except talking about the Cursers, not the Enchanters."

"'*You may be the Cursers' key to success,*'" I quoted. "He even went so far as to say that a Speaker had seen that Enchantia would fall."

The table gasped, and the atmosphere in the room suddenly turned anxious and worried.

"A-a Speaker said that?" Mr. Hudson raised his eyebrows at me. He looked terrified.

"Yeah, he said that a Speaker had guaranteed . . . the fall of Enchantia . . . "

Then, what I was saying hit me. Speakers were always right. When they had a vision about something or said a prophecy it *always* came true.

But . . . that meant that Enchantia would fall . . .

I couldn't afford to think like that.

Mrs. Cordelia shook her head. "For the moment, we will have to hope that he was lying." She looked over at Raven's empty chair. "A lot of Cursers lie."

It was silent for a minute, and then Mr. Hudson cleared his throat. "In other news, we have to thank you. We had guessed that someone was working for the Cursers before, but I would've never thought that it was Raven."

"And now that that's over," Ms. Maple continued, "we need you guys to continue, or start, training. I'm not a Speaker, but it's pretty obvious that something big is about to go down here. And we need all the help we can get."

"We'll do the best we can," I said. "I can promise you that. If what Casper said really is true, we're not going to go down easy."

CHAPTER 16

SURPRISES ALL AROUND

A lot happened over the next month.

I started my classes with Parker, Luna, and Mason. Austin and Daniel were actually a year older than the rest of us, so I would never have classes with them. That was also why they had the robes and Luna and Mason didn't. We would get ours next year.

Also unlike them, we didn't have multiple teachers. Our Leader was Mr. Everwood, the Healer Leader. He was pretty cool. Since the four of us were the only ones of our age there, we had his class all to ourselves. The only thing I wasn't a fan of was the fact that Early Magics didn't get to do actual magic classes yet. *Seriously*? But that did mean we got done with our classes earlier than everyone else, so that was a bonus.

I got closer with my new friends. Only a few days after we got back from our journey, it was time to decorate Enchantia for the holidays. One thing about the Enchanters: They go all out on their decorations. There was a giant Christmas tree in the common area, lights on the roof of the castle, and I kept running into dreidels on the tables. We made a day out of it, and no ornaments were harmed or broken in the decorating of the tree (cough, yeah right, Mason, cough). We spent evenings snow fighting, talking by the fireplaces in the common area, and watching movies in Austin's bedroom, which had a TV.

Austin, Parker, and I all went home for the holidays while Mason, Luna, and Daniel stayed at Enchantia. While I was at home, my parents gave me some good, but very unexpected, news.

I was lying sprawled out on my bed, having just finished the book I'd been reading the morning Casper first came after me. (Sure, there was a library at Enchantia, but I didn't remember what page I was on.) As I lay thinking about what had happened in the story, my mom stuck her head in the room.

"Hey, Evelyn," she walked in and sat down on my bed. I instantly put my book back in my drawer. "There's something we need to talk to you about."

Not good, I thought.

My dad walked in my room and sat down at my desk, facing me.

I was scared. "What is it?"

Immediately, my brain jumped to conclusions. Something had happened at Enchantia. The Cursers had kidnapped one of my friends. The island had collapsed. Enchantia had been attacked and someone had been badly hurt or worse.

I did not expect the answer that came out of Mom's mouth. "We've been thinking about adopting."

I stared at her, appalled. I was sure I'd misunderstood that. "You . . . you've been what?"

My dad slid the desk chair forward and put a hand on my shoulder. "Well, you see, there's a six year old girl in Boston we've been thinking about adopting. It turns out that she's an orphaned Enchanter, and, since you can't have an actual blood sibling, we've been thinking about adopting her. That is, as long as you're okay with it."

I just stared at them. How was I supposed to react to this?

Then I thought of Austin and how he had reacted to his little sister being claimed as the traitor. I thought of Luna and how much she missed her brother. I thought of Mason and how much hurt he had been through as an orphaned kid himself.

Now, I had the chance to save a kid like Mason. I could give them love the same way my friends had shown up out of nowhere and brought me happiness.

The better question was: *How could I refuse that?*

Tears started falling down my cheeks. I nodded, "Let's do it."

The next week, I went back to Enchantia. By the way, the day we went back, January 8th, was my 13th birthday.

They took us to the island on a riverboat much bigger than the original sailboat I'd traveled in with Parker and the Hunts. I found Parker and Austin on the boat, and we spent the entire ride talking about how our vacation had been.

I told them about the little girl, and Parker just gave me a goofy grin.

"What?" I asked her.

"Be careful," she warned, "Little sisters can be tiny demons."

I snorted, "I've always found that a weird comparison. There's no way they *actually* behave like that."

Parker raised her eyebrows. "I have *four* siblings, remember?"

That changed my mind and terrified me.

Soon, we were back at Enchantia, and I got another surprise, but this one I'd been kind of expecting.

We walked into the common area and found Mason, Luna, and Daniel sitting around a small coffee table near the fireplace on the right wall.

Mason was lounging in an armchair while Luna and Daniel were cuddling on a couch. We said our hellos, and the three of us sat down on the couch next to them.

Mason gave us a big grin. "Hey, give the lovebirds some space."

Parker raised her eyebrows. "What did you just call them?"

"You heard me right," he told her and pointed at Luna and

Daniel. "I caught these two lovebirds over here *kissing*."

Austin, Parker, and I burst out laughing.

Daniel glared at us. "Do you find that funny?"

I shook my head. "No, it's just . . . It was pretty obvious you guys liked each other."

"No, it wasn't," Luna argued.

"How about him giving you his robe when you were cold?" I said.

"How about the birthday cake?" Parker said.

"How about the fact that Daniel clearly knew the story about your brother before the rest of us?" Austin said.

"Okay, fine," Luna responded, "Maybe we made it a little obvious–"

"*A lot obvious,*" Mason corrected.

"A lot obvious, but the fact is we *do* like each other." Daniel kissed Luna on top of the head. "So now we're dating."

"*Finally,*" Mason grinned. "I'm going to have a lot of fun with this."

"Um, no you're not."

He laughed. "Oh, yes I am."

"Anyway," Luna interrupted, "speaking of birthdays, Mason?"

He grinned again and flicked his wrist.

A small box slid out from under the armchair. Another simple flick, and it soared up onto the coffee table.

"Open it," Parker said.

I reached forward and lifted the lid. Inside was a light blue cake, decorated to look like the ocean. In golden letters were the words *Happy Birthday, Evelyn!*

My friends burst out singing *Happy Birthday*. I couldn't help laughing at the unnecessary *cha cha cha*'s Mason and Parker were adding between the verses.

Lessons didn't start up until the next day, so we spent the day down at the pool: jumping off the diving board, having sword fights with pool noodles, playing games in the water. At one point, we pushed Luna and Daniel in the pool. Because, you know, when your friends start dating you can't leave them alone.

At the end of the day, I went back to my room in good spirits. As a little treat to myself, I decided to read the sequel to the book I'd been reading before.

I fingered through the books, trying to remember where I'd seen it. I finally found it and pulled it out, but another book came with it and fell onto the ground.

I bent down to pick it up and realized that it wasn't one of my fantasies.

It was the notebook I'd written in after I left my house.

I picked it up, sat on my bed, and read through it. It was like reliving everything that had happened. But I'd never gotten to finish it . . .

I glanced at the clock on my bedside table. It wasn't that late. Surely I could spend just a little bit of time on it?

I bounded across my room, sat down on my desk chair, picked up a pencil, and began to write.

My adventures weren't over, that much was clear to me. Luna's brother and Ava were still missing, Enchantia was a Leader short, and some Speaker out there was predicting the fall of the Enchanters.

But, for the moment, I was happy. I was going to be a big sister. I was being accepted for my autism. I was going to a magic school.

Most importantly, I had friends.

Things weren't going to magically improve. We had tons of problems ahead of us. But, as long as we had each other, things would turn out alright in the end.

Or would it?

Remember when Luna said that Speakers weren't always shown bad things because they may try to stop them?

Well, let's just say there's a reason none of our Speakers saw anything . . .

ABOUT

THE AUTHOR

My name is Makayla Sperle, I'm a fourteen-year-old with Autism who decided to become an author at a very young age. I've been reading for as long as I can remember, and it has been a lifelong dream of mine to publish a book.

In my spare time, I enjoy swimming (which majorly inspired the book), reading, writing, traveling, and hanging out with friends. It is a great joy to me that I was able to write this book about the things I love most.

Made in the USA
Middletown, DE
05 December 2023

44572752R00106